Superwomen

Superwomen

Inspiring Stories of
20 Women Entrepreneurs

Prachi Garg

Srishti
PUBLISHERS & DISTRIBUTORS

Srishti Publishers & Distributors
Registered Office: N-16, C.R. Park
New Delhi – 110 019
Corporate Office: 212A, Peacock Lane
Shahpur Jat, New Delhi – 110 049
editorial@srishtipublishers.com

First published by
Srishti Publishers & Distributors in 2016

10 9 8 7 6 5

Disclaimer: This is a work of non-fiction, charting the stories of twenty women entrepreneurs and their start-ups. All the stories and pictures herein have been narrated and given to the author by the person concerned and have been reproduced herein with their due permission. Although the author and publisher have made every effort to ensure that the information in this book was correct at press time, the author and publisher do not assume and hereby disclaim any liability to any party for any loss, damage, or disruption caused by errors or omissions, whether such errors or omissions result from negligence, accident, or any other cause.

Printed and bound in India

Dedicated to my parents.
I owe this success completely to them.

Contents

Acknowledgements

This book has been possible due to the enormous love and support that people have given to me. It was their constant support that kept me going and ensured that I should be able to deliver it on time. I would like to thank the following people to make this journey smooth for me.

My father, Mr. Brejesh Garg, who has been a constant support to me and inspired me at every step.

My mother, Neeru Garg, who motivated me whenever I lost hope and got tired.

My siblings Himadri Garg and Anant Garg, who read each chapter and gave their critical feedback.

My husband, Nitin Gupta, who made sure I don't get disturbed while writing it.

My friends Amrita Marik and Smruti, who guided me at every step of publishing.

Shrishti Publishers for putting faith in my concept and agreeing to publish it.

All my friends who gave me constant moral support to make this happen.

And finally, all the entrepreneurs who took out time and shared their brilliant stories with me, so that I could share it with you all.

I hope you all get inspired with their journey and contribute to the progress of the nation.

Medhavi Gandhi *founded* **Happy Hands** *to revive traditional/ folk art and craft with an aim to empower rural artisans and hone potential in women and young people.*

The Revival of Art, Culture and a Country

Medhavi Gandhi

India is a country full of history, art and culture. Every corner sprouts a variety of creativity – both subtle and profound. The families of artisans have carried it on for generations. And yet, when the son of a lac bangle maker in a small village says he doesn't want to carry on the family craft, not be a bangle maker like his father, it does not come as a surprise. Thousands of artisans across the country have been forced to look for alternate sources of income, many compelled to give up their art altogether because their hard work did not reach socio-economic recognition for bare minimum sustenance. While many may stop to consider this loss of national heritage for a moment before turning their attention towards the commercially potent and prominent products in the market, a very small handful of people halt for a little longer. A shining example of the latter is Medhavi Gandhi, a young and dynamic activist who has emerged as a reformist, dedicated to provide a sustainable platform for artisans.

At the young age of twenty-two, the art enthusiast started what she thought was a movement to promote local artists and fast dying traditional forms of craft, especially in the rural areas of the country. Ask her what brought her to this road, and you will realize that it has been a journey of internal reasoning and external observations. As an eager learner, Medhavi interned in some of the most insightful environments, the most significant of which turned out to be her experience in UNESCO.

"I increasingly encountered situations which forced me to realize that while the youth potential of India was huge, their awareness and recognition of Indian arts, crafts and heritage was embarrassingly low. This of course included me because our education system was such. Though we train to be doctors, engineers, and MBAs, nobody trains to be a traditional artisan – designer yes, artisan, no," she expresses vehemently.

This became the motivation to create a platform where the undeniably dying art of the country can be exposed and evolved to an audience to reclaim its appreciation and existence. The basic idea was born out of the distress of the artisans who were forced to sell their products not at the value of their effort and skill but at throwaway prices that was threatening their mere survival. "I knew right away this is what I had to work for. This was something I dived into right after completing my education," explains the English honours graduate who has specialized in Master's in communication. On the way to finding, meeting and promoting colloquial artists, Medhavi crossed paths with many women, a lot of them from foreign countries, residing in the hearts of cities and towns across the country, dedicating their lives to the causes of the eclipsing heritage. Committed to their service, these foreigners had learnt the local language to communicate better. All this was more than inspiring for a young Medhavi to bring together her motivation and resources into an amalgamation of art and business, with a vision of creating happiness for those who create and engage in art, known today as Happy Hands.

Somewhere between her movement, Medhavi encountered what had been the endeavours of the world-renowned Kamla Devi Chattopadhyay, who contributed immensely in giving the country a perspective strong enough to form the National School of Drama, the Craft Council and the Performing Arts Museum. This motivated the dynamic leader into institutionalizing her vision into a forum that could not only be recognized as a gateway for all forms of artefacts but also provided for linking the craft with its rightful value in a demand and supply chain.

"In 2009, we worked across villages with artists, and marketed their products in the city tirelessly. In 2010, we started workshops and public interventions to enable the public to interact with the artisans. It was something we saw as imperative to boost the perception of folk art," explains the insightful entrepreneur.

The mobilization of the enterprise happened through collaboration of friends and well-wishers who believed in Medhavi's cause and concern. While she confesses to having no knowledge of the social sector, the legal system and commercial liaising in the initial stages, Medhavi acclaims the contributions of her associations who came in the form of legal advisors, volunteers supporting market linkages, company registration and even fund flow were immense. "This was also the time we strengthened our relationship with multiple corporates and were given interesting work – using folk arts for promotions, communication, or simply as gifts!" she explains the strategic growth of Happy Hands.

And hence, with the help of a dedicated team of employees, volunteers, interns and contributors, Happy Hands found itself expanding and diversifying into different means for promotion of art and craft of the country. From workshops, to engaging in art, to corporate linkages for product supplies; from the innovation of a residency studio of art for artists, to a platform of education of heritage to rural and urban population that would lead to academic absorption and promotion of heritage art – Happy Hands is spreading its reach with the passing of each milestone.

Though things have streamlined and focused into what looks like an institution in itself, Happy Hands has seen its days of challenges and hurdles too. "There were times we faced a severe financial crunch," confesses an honest Medhavi. "We needed to bring together an efficient staff but often found ourselves at a loss of funds."

Learning through the tough times, Happy Hands floated with volunteers and interns in its more critical moments, a support Medhavi continues to accredit and employ even today. Not having sufficient experience with entrepreneurial management also made things a major challenge to bring together artists from different backgrounds together and convince them to collaborate for the enterprise. "It took me a while to bring the artists into an enterprising mode, through workshops, training; it was a long process to bring together this platform to a convincing standard."

Being an off-beat business idea has had its own trials. Not only are small and individual suppliers of products hard to convince, but even more so, dealing with fraudsters who conveniently target women-based businesses thinking they would get by easy has been a challenge. However, not easily discouraged, Medhavi has learnt her lessons well in the world of business and continues to accept such challenges graciously.

Overcoming the hurdles of initial uncertainties was what has brought the artist at heart this far with her passion, "My parents have always pushed my limits and stood by me. Initially, they were only a little worried about my financial health…but understood soon enough that I was too charged up to bother about finance." The support that has come to Medhavi in the form of volunteers and friends is what has kept her encouraged and persistent in the trying times, she acknowledges heartily. "Today, we have a strong bond with both the artists and the customers of art, we surely have come a long way in the process of building of the original objective," she accepts with a humble glint in her eyes. Having started with a core team of three members, today Happy Hands stands strong with seven permanent employees and a bouquet of talents in the form of interns and volunteers from all disciplines of education and experience to help them grow.

"In the course of running an organization, I have learnt how to budget, recruit, design, travel on minimal resources, and how to function with no sleep, but occasional dreams. By most importantly, I have learnt about people and their traditions and cultures," she sums up the essence of Happy Hands in just that one sentence.

Travelling through the cross section of cities across the country and diving deep into the rural synergy of the states has brought out an entirely new perspective in the compassionate observer that Medhavi is.

"We connect with the artists over a cup of tea at most times," she springs candidly at the hint of the subject. Spilling with passion and excitement of stories she has witnessed through the many roads travelled, Medhavi talks about her strategy of collaboration with artists as one based on relationships.

"Once we have narrowed a region and its art, it's all about understanding the artists, their culture and building a bond with them. That's the essence that takes the business a long way, not numbers and figures," reveals the insightful artist. Training and capacity building with the artisans through ice-breaking and enterprise discussions has been the backbone of supporting both the artists as well as Medhavi in discovering newer potentials and possibilities within each segment of art.

Spending most of her time in villages with the craftsmen, the high-spirited entrepreneur loves living under the stars, where she believes real life breathes. Dividing her days between corporate workshops, meetings and collaborations in the city on the one hand, and easing her way through the hard work of training and ensuring quality support to artists in their home ground on the other, make up Medhavi's calendar. Strumming her guitar once in a while or sauntering her paint brush with water colours also keeps the inner artist alive, a habit she has nurtured effortlessly through the years. With over five years of leading a movement and heading an organization, Medhavi has clearly ripened with sensitivity and inspiration that eulogizes her enterprise. Feeling passionately for the artists she works with, the business woman also associates her moments of pride and success with the benchmarks of their achievements. "I felt it when Om Prakash entered the Limca Book of Records; I felt it when Chinniyachari went to Moscow; I felt it when Sandhya Devi bagged a state award; and I felt it when Radha went back to her craft after her wedding and taught her husband too!" she exults with pride.

Having climbed to heights that she had started scudding at from a very young age, the bright finalist for the Rolex Award for Enterprise already has her mind set to the next goal. While expansion in terms of geography and scale are a top agenda for Happy Hands, educating people about the heritage of the country and increasing the capacity of the ancient skills is what Medhavi aims at giving an organized boost through Happy Hands. With a team consistently growing, corporate endorsements commercially rising and a reputation being recognized, the enterprise not only stands to fulfill its set goals in the near future, but is also keen to attain the status of a game changer in the verticals of the art and craft industry of the country.

To be able to identify one's passion and feel it burning under one's skin can be found in plenty of high spirited explorers of the world. But to find a cause that can potentially turn around history and to make that one's passion is something worth learning from the vibrant Medhavi Gandhi. With a practical start from scratch, not only has she brought Happy Hands, her entrepreneurial baby, up to its extraordinary growth in the last five years, but in the process has also created a stage for the artists of the country to find new dimensions of not mere revival or sustenance, but what may evolve to become a revolutionary trend changer. Envisaging a socio-economic prosperity where a son doesn't have to be embarrassed about his father's craft, Medhavi is close enough to inspire a restoration of the art and heritage of the country which was on the brink of a silent demise. Combining her passion with a commercially lucrative blend, Happy Hands is an example many aspiring entrepreneurs can learn and be inspired by.

Do your bit in preserving traditional art and craft. Join hands with Happy Hands at www.happyhands.in.

Ria Sharma *(right) with Monica, one of the acid attack survivors who was helped by* **Make Love Not Scars**, *an NGO that works to stop acid attacks and other forms of gender-based violence, along with supporting the survivors.*

Beauty – More than Skin Deep

Ria Sharma

She was a girl with a happy life, with the privilege of a good lifestyle and education. With the best make-up on, she stepped outside her house each day and found her way into her stepmother's jewellery design store where she worked amidst shiny trinkets. A job every girl dreams of. She went off to England to study fashion in one of the best universities of the world. She lived a life most people would call luxurious, and yet, explored its many facets. But it was hard for her to submit to what her professors asked of her and what she really thought and did. Clearly, things weren't going the way they were supposed to. Nobody for the longest time even understood what she was doing, seeing or thinking. Some thought this was a phase; others believed her to have digressed from her expected course of action. And then, she emerged from the dilemma, outshone all expectations that were doing the rounds and set on a journey that would go on to change many lives, and most importantly, change her own life in dimensions she hadn't even imagined existed.

The twenty-one-year-old of Leeds College of Art was struggling through her projects in fashion. She had tried and pretended, and forced and failed to find any cognizance of her spirit with the conventional definitions of fashion. She knew her heart was not in it. Therefore, when the final project of the last semester came upon the young girl, she was flustered with the lack of choice or motivation and a desperate need to come up with something. She would otherwise surely fail! That was when she really dug deep into her heart to find what she really wanted. Irrespective of whether it had to do with conventional sense of fashion or not, Ria discovered what her heart yearned for.

"I have always felt very strongly for the condition of women in India. I even worked on a project with rape victims. I knew I would cross paths with issues related to women empowerment, but I hadn't imagined it would come in this shape and depth," she talks about the initiation of her project.

"My professors thankfully helped me improvise when they figured I couldn't be pinned down by conventional genres for my project. The subject of acid attacks was consuming me and I knew I had to work my project around it, and I did!"

Coming back to India for research and documentation of her final project was a blessing in disguise for the young crusader. She went around the country recording instances, experiences and consequences of acid attacks on women. And what she encountered changed her perspective towards everything in life. It turned out to be a visual experience that set the path of her determination that became her life, her passion, and even her career.

"It had merely begun as a college project. I wanted to break conventions and work on something I could relate to. Although I had very little knowledge about the survivors of acid attacks back then, the journey consumed me with one experience after another. I knew I would never be the same again."

Ria's name for her endeavours reflected deeply about what she wanted to express. A project related to fashion she was working on required that she come up with something creative. She wanted to work on something relevant and uplifting for herself and all the women she was representing through the project.

"Make Love Not Scars was intended to be the intention and identity of the project at the outset. Although I did see a few raised eyebrows for coming up with something like this, we were determined to go ahead with it. Today, it stands in itself as a name we all are proud of, as it encourages to spread love and happiness, and embrace who we are," Ria says.

Speaking of her inspiration, Ria shares her experience in Bangalore with an acid attack activist, Haseena, who had overcome several struggles and opposition – social, financial and medical. Despite having been blinded by an attack on herself, the bold fighter had guided many survivors and provided protection and care. As a young student, there was a lot for Ria to learn and understand and it was primarily Haseena who guided her through the processes. From understanding the situation of the survivors, to learning about the legal, medical, financial, social or emotional aspects of acid attacks and what it meant to support such survivors, Ria took small yet significant steps to embracing each of these hard hitting facts.

"There were times when I thought I had had enough and didn't want to go meet another person. It was during these times that Haseena held my hand and provided me with the strength I needed to go on and pursue the cause," she reveals with gratitude.

Delving deep into the world of information, Ria made strength of her heart and learnt as much as she could about the laws, medical facilities and financial requirements that revolved around an acid attack survivor. She visited hospitals, witnessed some of the most gruesome acts forced on the survivors. The more she saw, the more it fuelled her determination towards her stand to support the cause. Make Love Not Scars became a purpose and platform for women from across the country to reach out and avail support in different forms. Today, hundreds of survivors have found support and shelter in the organization and a plethora of supporters from India and across the world have come together in spirit and in action to fight for the cause – spreading awareness, creating campaigns and reaching out to victims.

While at a glance, Make Love Not Scars may simply appear to be a philanthropic organization supporting women with a history of acid attacks, it has deeper layers of underlying struggles and implications. Many of those Ria has fought through and overcome today, and yet plentiful she battles with every single day. The struggle to be taken seriously by her funders and partners was a challenge. Because of her age and appearance, Ria was presumed to be inexperienced. Being able to align her passion for the cause with organizational requirements and funds was also a challenge that Ria had to slowly learn to tackle. However, these hurdles were external barriers. The biggest challenge was what was transforming inside Ria. Once she delved deep into the history of the cases, it was impossible for her to get back to her normal life, pretending to engage her mind in the superficial, insignificant activities.

"Initially my family did not understand the state of mind that I was in; they thought it was a phase I was going through. I would be with them but my heart would never leave the faces I had seen. It was like being torn into a different person, someone I hadn't met before," she recalls. After making the decision to work in the area, Ria also had to overcome the inner turmoil. Her brush with the lives of survivors in the beginning often left her squeamish and scared. This was a battle she had to fight with herself to be able to embrace the pain and horror that the acid attack victims had been through.

"I thought I was going to save them. But I eventually realized they were the ones saving me. They were rescuing me from all the material, inconsequential and superficial engagements of life. They were helping me embrace my own identity, my own existence with pride."

Her voice resonates a strength rarely seen for a woman of her age. Ria's pledge to go make-up free 365 days is a vivid example of how she had internalized the cause.

"I was someone who would cake on make-up every time I stepped out. Whether I was meeting friends, going to college or simply shopping, my face always had a layer of make-up because I had issues appreciating my face just the way it was. Even when I went to meet the acid attack survivors, I had my make up on," she confesses. As someone who was telling survivors to drop the veil of their physical appearance and embrace who they were, Ria realized her hypocrisy and shed that last strip of superficial attachment by pledging to wear no make-up at all for a year. The entire process was not only a strengthening eye opener for her, but also a source of motivation for the members of her organization who felt more comfortable in practicing what she was endorsing.

Having found her inspiration in the fighting spirit of the survivors, Ria continued her advocacy and campaigns in an attempt to reach out in every possible incident. During her research, she had come across a mother and child who had been burnt in a brutal acid attack. Back then, she had tried her level best as a student to get help and to raise any aid possible for the victims, but failed.

"If Make Love Not Scars had existed at that time, I know I could have helped them. I know they would have lived. I don't want to see that happening to anyone else anymore," she adds determined.

Everything she had ever learnt, from her experiences to her education, Ria has poured into her cause for supporting survivors. Through her modules of fashion communication, she learnt how to express the vivid experiences in a way that the audience can relate to and contribute, right from shooting experiences of her survivors, editing the photos and creating campaigns.

"A part of my degree revolved around social media skills. We had an entire module dedicated to social media, and at the time, I didn't think I would use it, but now most of my funding comes through the internet," she shares.

Having come this far and making continued progress, Ria has helped the organization reach out to many, partner up with several funding organizations and connect many to be a contributive part of the cause.

"Currently, Make Love Not Scars is teamed by twelve core members and an entire pod of volunteers from across different disciplines of expertise. Along with that, some of the survivors have also risen to join us in the cause and are now active participants in our daily activities. When the need arises, someone or the other always steps in to contribute in their relevant field. A lot of support comes silently, while for some, a lot of awareness is created, depending on the objective of the mission at hand." Ask her what she has to say about the success she has achieved at such a young age and Ria shies away with all humility. "I will call myself successful the day I know that not a single survivor of acid attacks in this country has gone without support. Till then, the fight is on."

With voracious plans of expansion, she speaks of forthcoming collaborations with excitement and hope they change the scale and effect of Make Love Not Scars significantly. But for her, every little step counts and every bit of progress is a moment of pride and passion. Her dedication can be seen in the words of those who have witnessed her working.

"She takes care of every survivor as family. When needed, she spends nights in the hospital to take care of those undergoing treatment and remains in touch even after they are discharged," says Bharat Nayak, founding member of The Logical Indian.

From being a self-conscious student studying appearances to a dynamic fighter who works hard to help women shed the boundaries of their looks, Ria has come a long way. For her close friends and family, witnessing her journey both professionally as well as personally has been an inspiration. She would engage in superficial, social engagements with a craving to be a part of everything that was going on. She would want to be perceived in a certain fashion. But the new, strong and steady Ria is someone who barely has time to float through inconsequential and mundane aspects of life that women her age generally relate to. Appreciating everything she has and dedicating everything in her power for a purpose that is much larger than her personal desires and ambitions, the avid activist has internalized the cause of Make Love Not Scars to the core of her being. Sending a shout-out to every person aspiring to break conventions and build something for their own or for the good of the larger cause, she says, "If you have a vision, hold onto it, work on it, nurture it and don't give up."

It is with this poignant determination that Ria has been changing lives one step after another and stands today as an example for people to learn from.

Volunteer to support and encourage acid attack survivors. Visit: www.makelovenotscars.com.

Richa Singh *founded* **Your D.O.S.T** *to provide online counselling and support system to anyone in need through trained individuals.*

Your Friend in Need

Richa Singh

After she acquired her premium degree from one of the top engineering colleges of the country, her parents had clearly not foreseen the choice she would be making a few years down the line. Her friends, who had watched her rise and fall through the different phases of her life, had not imagined this would be the step she would take in her attempt to bring things to an end. And yet, amidst the doubts, challenges and apprehensions, Richa came out as a winner to pursue a career that not only brought her on the path to discover the purpose of her life, but also brought about the creation of a world which has gone on to change the lives of many for the better. In a fiercely competitive and self-centred world where almost everyone is stuck feeling alone in the crowd of many, she has brought hope and companionship into the lives of those who need it the most.

Having graduated from IIT Guwahati, Richa, like the many top students of the country started her career with some of the most established organizations. With a high package, a stable job and a family who was proud of her, our young and dynamic sports enthusiast had no complaints to make. Except that her mind wandered into seeking something deeper and more meaningful.

Her switch to join a start-up came as a surprise to everyone who knew her. "Why would you leave everything for something you don't even know well?" her friends and family tried to reason. But Richa knew where her heart was. She spent the four years grappling with the challenges faced by start-ups. Building organizations from scratch, growing from a team of five to a global organization, learning all the nuances of the business were all incentives no money could measure up. It is here then, with gained experience and motivated capacity, that she set out to work on the dream she had dreamed of many years ago.

As an engineering aspirant preparing for entrances in Kota, Richa had first-hand experience watching people around her collapsing due to stress and pressure of their careers, emotions and expectations.

"Watching a close friend go through severe depression and having to deal with it all by himself made me feel very helpless. I really wish there was someone out there who could have helped him out," she recollects.

Desperation arose in her and it kept her restless in search of a way she could help those who could not find any resort. While in a spiritual and practical search for answers, an incident occurred in her life that changed Richa's perspective and motivation for ever.

"During graduation, a friend, who had been going through severe anxiety owing to her job placement, committed suicide one random evening. I had never even realized that she had been going through so much stress. All I could think of was that she could have been saved." That was the turning point of Richa's quest. From being a bystander and mourner, her heart was set on finding a solution and doing whatever she could to save people from their states of stress, anxiety or depression. One fine morning, when the thought could not contain itself any more, she broke all shackles of comfort, quit her job, and started to build what has now become to engage and inspire many people across the country, her enterprise – Your D.O.S.T.

In a world that caters to material needs of people, Richa set out to serve as an emotional support system. "I know what it feels like to be emotionally wrecked. It feels lonely and one feels lost, and that's when you need a true and responsible friend," she sums up the ethos of Your D.O.S.T. It is a service that enables people to vent out their problems, discuss them anonymously with compassionate and non-judgmental individuals. Through Your D.O.S.T, Richa offers a listening ear to people who may be going through emotional crises but are too apprehensive to seek professional help or discuss about the same.

"The entire taboo about seeking psychological help is what commonly prevents people from getting help when they need it most," explains Richa with years of experience now. To address this big challenge, she designed her enterprise as a friend anyone can confide in. It creates a virtual environment which can be accessed from anywhere, without disclosing one's identity. It also further provides peer to peer discussions so people can share and learn from each other. "Without judgement or opinion, like your very own friend who helps you get informed counsel, Your D.O.S.T. stands by you with honesty and trust – something very hard to find these days," she expresses the fundamental principle of her venture.

A fan of the American sitcom series, Richa has felt the connection you can form with your reliable friends. It is also what inspired her to name her enterprise keeping in true spirit with everything that Your D.O.S.T. is supposed to entail. If one wonders what got her to choose such an unusual name and path for her career, her surprise is not concealed at all. "Oh this is not offbeat!

A need for friend is so obvious and so it feels like the most obvious thing to do considering the needs of today's times."

Happy to have made that choice, Richa now works on building what has not only been her dream, but her motivation for life. With fond partnership and support from her now very good friends Puneet and Satyajeet, also the co-founders of Your D.O.S.T, her resolution has come a long way into becoming a full-fledged emotional support system.

"From the day I told Satyajeet about the idea, he started coding to prepare the interface for us. Puneet, on the other hand, started working on building a sustainable business model around the idea. We make a good and dedicated team together. We all come from very different skillsets, but one thing that runs across all three of us is the compassion and the drive to help others," states Richa with satisfaction.

What may seem like a successful and smooth running platform today has seen its share of challenges along the way. Recalling her fight for the foundation, Richa confesses to having no illusion that this was going to be an easy ride at all! Starting an enterprise as a woman was not easy for her in the first go. Having a self start-up, and especially dealing with an unconventional theme, raised many eye brows. "My family was not excited about the idea in the initial phase. They thought getting married was a far better option than walking blindly towards a career with no certain path or steady income," she reveals with a hint of a smile. "But they saw how determined I was about this, and frankly I wasn't giving them a choice!" Heading a venture in the field of psychology, without her having any background of the subject also posed a considerable challenge for the aspiring entrepreneur.

"I spent a lot of time researching on the issue, and spending time through visits or calls with the experts to strengthen my understanding. The first and foremost challenge that brought itself before me was looking for a developer who could not only understand the need of Your D.O.S.T, but also someone who was sensitive about the issue. After meeting a lot of people, bumping into Satyajeet came as a blessing.

"The team is the backbone of Your D.O.S.T. and it took us a while to put all the members together," she says remembering the initial days.

But turning challenges into opportunity has been the signature style for the go-getter Richa. When they were on the look-out for people, many volunteers and well wishers spilled their love and support to help the team out generously. Experimentation and persistent trial has been the leading lady's mantra. Through the endeavours, she has put her education and knowledge about user behaviour to good use.

"I employed every bit of my sensibility from my experience with start-ups. I was prepared for the failures and open to making mistakes. I knew these would turn into my strength," she exonerates with confidence. "The first signs of success came when people cast aside their shells of apprehension and reached out to us for support. We knew we were on the right path that very moment. There has been no looking back since."

A content and distant gaze of the passionate thinker betrays her emotional involvement with her avocation. Feeling satisfied with the differences she has made in people's life, she reflects on the hopes lost in past years.

"I wish I had started earlier; there were so many more who we could have reached out to."

Finding close cognizance with times when emotional support is desperately needed, Richa shares experiences that have shaken and shaped her from the inside. "A rape victim reached out to us and felt a lot lighter after the contact. It's not that we can go back and undo what happened, but it's a relief to know that she sleeps better now. There is a case of a guy from a small town who felt free to discuss his sexuality openly with us. He had earlier believed he was alone in the world." These little moments go on to reveal a lot about the impact Your D.O.S.T has been creating on silently suffering lives across the country. For each call connected, there's hope for a life-changing experience for the user and that's what makes Your D.O.S.T more than just a business or some individual's passion.

Having crossed the first thousand user mark in the first few weeks of operations, the support venture has a fan following well recognized across the table. They raised funds amounting to rupees five lakhs with backing from a hundred and twenty well-wishers through Milaap. An exemplary endeavour, Your D.O.S.T. has also been proudly featured by the *Huffington Post* in the the article 'Seven ordinary people doing extraordinary things' – a recognition that speaks volumes for the start-up. All set with plans of expansion, Richa claims the organization's aim is to become a platform catering to India specific needs as she believes this is a country that faces a gamut of challenges and requires special attention.

"I want Your D.O.S.T. to be available and understood by people far and wide in the country, even in the remotest areas. We need to break the shackles of taboo we have built around seeking psychological support in India, and that's what I am setting out to do. We want to enable more and more people to be able to talk about their feelings to non-judgmental people without any fear, and in turn feel better," her confidence resonates in her words and passion.

These aspirations help and evolve Richa both professionally and personally in her world. A regular Yoga practitioner, she believes firmly in taking risks and embracing failures with as much grace as she does victories. As an individual, she believes in keeping her body as fit as her mind. Waking up early in the morning, practicing her Pranayams help to keep her centreed and focused through the day. A budget traveller, an avid reader and a dedicated foodie, Richa also nurtures her passion for sports. Living each day of her life with enthusiasm and harmony, she embodies a sense of belonging for the entire cosmos around her.

As an inspiration to the ambitious, aspiring or even apprehensive women entrepreneurs of the country, Richa today stands tall as an example of building passion and compassion into profession. While reinstating her faith in the strength of women, she believes that mutual support and respect can take womankind a long way. She also sends out a strong message to bring the men and boys of the country to be completely conscious about respect for women. As someone who closely encounters the challenges both men and women face in times of emotional crisis, Richa believes that equal and empathetic conduct towards one another can work as the best friend one needs in the world. Changing lives of many who thought they had lost hope, friendship and trust, she goes on to revamp the foundations of the society that have begun to weaken out of ignorance and indifference.

Masoom Minawala's *passion for fashion led to her brain-child* **Style Fiesta**, *an online destination for trendy fashion jewellery and accessories.*

She Works in Style!

Masoom Minawala

The tomboy who walked down her school, the football champion who captained her team and the tardy teenager who came home with the dirtiest socks, this young spirited girl was someone her mother chided for her blatant ignorance of her feminine instincts. That such a girl would pick up fashion magazines at the prime of her teens and take a liking to them was unlikely. What was even more unlikely is that she would go on to pursue her interest in fashion both in her education, as well as her career. For someone who knew her as a tomboy in school, it would be impossible to imagine how she butterflied into being a famous, loved and well-accomplished fashion expert across the world. And yet, all of the most unlikely things did happen and left the onlookers awe-inspired.

Born and brought up in the boisterous city of Mumbai, Masoom displayed shades of interest that varied between high energy sports to indulgent research on fashion magazines. As she took the expected course of action and went on to pursue her Bachelor's degree in commerce, it was an amalgamation of her interest in fashion and her desire to intern productively that brought her in close contact with the actual world of fashion, outside of fashion magazines and into fashion houses. This began with an internship in her cousin's production house.

"I have to admit, I got to know within the first fourteen days of the work that I was not made for this!" she exclaims candidly. Having made progress through elimination, Masoom moved on to her next experience in one of the best brand marketing organizations, only this time to handle the business aspect of the style world. One of her projects with the brand was involving fashion bloggers. This is where she had her first brush with the phenomenal concept. For her, it was love at first sight! Having explored and understood the dynamics of commercial blogging, the young learner, fresh out of college, started her own blog on fashion.

"I used to write about styling and experimenting with one's existing wardrobe, getting my mom and aunt to photograph for me and put it online. I even experimented with a lot of self-portraits," she explains. In love with the concept of expression of various styles on the internet, Masoom continued to express her fashion perspectives for the whole world to see.

But the real game changers came at her desktop when the mere hobby of writing by the fashionista started getting noticed in the form of hits, comments and feedback from readers across the world. "Just like that, I was connecting with faceless names from different parts of the country. We started building a relationship with the exchange of ideas. They liked what I wrote, many even adopted my ideas. That's when I knew things were going to get wider from fun blogging to business," she recollects.

About two years into blogging, Masoom had identified the opportunities and gaps in the online fashion space just waiting to be tapped. "I had travelled outside the country with my parents and had realized there was a huge gap between international fashion and what the Indian perception of international fashion was. This is the gap I wanted to bridge," she speaks in a tone of determination. Working hard on the foundation of her work, Masoom took the insightful advice of her father who encouraged her to take formal education in the world of fashion before diving into it fulltime.

"I had no formal training in fashion; I knew that was one area I needed to strengthen. My only experience had been through fashion magazines and my brief experience with the brands I interned with." Thus the decision to move to London and pursue formal education in the London College of Fashion & Central Saint Martins for six diploma courses in the Business of Fashion was taken. This not only prepared the fashion enthusiast into handling the business aspect of a potentially massive venture, but also exposed her to further opportunities and styles that inspired her in the coming years.

After the completion of her course, Masoom returned to Mumbai and immediately got down to working around her idea of an online venture. Hence emerged the platform that offered attractive, affordable and accessible fashion from across the world. Fondly named Stylefiesta.com, the enterprise went live in December 2012. Masoom positioned the e-commerce venture from the very beginning with aspirations of large scale and reach. She did not want Style Fiesta to be confined to any single vicinity.

"My aim was and continues to be to bring fashion to anyone who wants it. The bigger cities of India like Mumbai and Delhi have access to the international brands and a variety of global fashion. But why should the smaller cities be deprived?" she questions challengingly. Having established herself as a loved and followed in fashion knowledge, it was smart and comfortable for the young entrepreneur to market the fashion ranges. The result?

Style Fiesta today has hundreds and thousands of customers from across the country, ranging from big metropolitan cities to small towns where no fashion brands have reached yet!

"I receive mails from my readers who switched to buying my products saying now they have their own fashion statements in their closets and not just in fashion magazines because of me! What more do I need?" she speaks with excitement.

Not having limited herself to the confinement of retail stores in only selected areas, Masoom talks proudly about being able to reach her customers at any place and time, on any occasion, with just a click. Talking about her target audience, the passionate writer defines them to be women between sixteen to thirty years of age, anyone who is enthusiastic about fashion.

"I am my target audience, you see," she explains categorically, "which is why I can absolutely understand what they are looking for, and whether they will like something or not. Having an idea about the perspective of my customers is a big help."

Speaking of her business model, she talks about the detailed process of handpicking about twenty products as a trial. "I wanted to see whether I could convert my readers into customers. I uploaded images; some styled on me, some product shots, along with prices and put down the payment method as a bank transfer. We were sold out in less than twenty-four hours!"

This leap of faith taken by her followers was proof enough for Masoom to know the idea had hit the jackpot. It was only a matter of time before her online portal was flooded with orders and requests. There has been no looking back since. Currently generating revenue from two platforms, the entrepreneur exemplifies a blend between creativity and commerce. While her popular blog works through collaborations with brands for promotions, her own product outlet, Style Fiesta is her stage for direct business.

On the path to building her own business, the dynamic leader went through her share of challenges and learning. But the optimist does admit to having made the most out of the hurdles and problems as such instances have made her stronger, both as an entrepreneur as well as an individual. "When people have something to say about your company, you've got to stick your head out and hear it. It could be good or it could be bad, but if you're looking at creating a product that's amazing, you need to hear the bad and transform it into something good," she speaks in reference to negative criticism. Speaking of funding challenges as well as the mistakes that have occurred in the process of this phenomenal growth, one might wonder if Masoom ever gets flustered.

"Never." She adds without a doubt, "If I had a chance to go back in time and do this any other way, I'd still do this exactly like this, with all the mistakes. I have learnt so much and I am so proud of it!" she exclaims.

Talking about things that have brought her this far in pursuit of her passion, Masoom expresses her awe in the power of the internet – the backbone of her enterprise. "The moment I realized I had the power to influence people around me with what I said, what I did and what I wore, I knew I was doing something right." Having found unconditional support in her family and friends, Masoom acknowledges the gratitude she feels for all the strength, criticism and improvement they have offered in the course of her career. Giving due credit to the hardworking team she has put together with time and evolution, she speaks humbly.

"Every single person who has ever been a part of Style Fiesta, whether it is the team members, collaborated brands, critics or customers, they are the ones who have brought me this far in actualizing the dream," she speaks with humility. Working currently with an effective team of fifteen members, Masoom has categorized the enterprise fairly into the major disciplines of an organization including, marketing, accounts, SEM, IT and warehousing. "We are a close-knit team, working hard to make things simple and effective."

As someone who lives her passion day and night, Masoom is an embodiment of what Style Fiesta stands for: sharing of style, elegance and joy with everyone. A passionate reader, she indulges in her avid interests of dance and photography when at home. Keeping a healthy balance, she also practices yoga and spends time with her family just with as much commitment as her dedicated hours at the headquarters. "It's been like a dream come true for me. It feels fantastic to have built something from scratch and brought it this far," she expresses with an elated smile. Counting her proud moments, she shares her feelings about the first comment on her blog, the first order, the first positive feedback, the first newspaper article, and the first shoot for a magazine. Every single day at office where she works with her entire team towards delivering accessible fashion to aspiring girls everywhere is her haven. Little achievements mean a lot more to the satiated fashionista. In sync with her current stature, Masoom plans to expand her brand and work by diversifying into further genres. Having already begun with the execution, the brand has already launched its range of bags and shoes, exciting many loyal customers. But of course this marks only the beginning of a buffet of trendy collections that is due to embrace the Indian market soon.

As someone who has risen on her own feet, as a woman entrepreneur in a primarily male dominated space, Masoom resonates confidence and inspires many young women to follow their dreams and passion despite the hindrances and challenges that wait in their paths.

"If anything, we're blessed with an undeniable charm that the opposite sex lacks, and we'd be foolish to not make use of it," she adds with a laugh. As a business woman who has risen against all odds, all conventional expectations and myths about herself, she sets an example for many women to cherish and follow. With her passion and dedication, she has reached out to women across the country in a scenario where a fashionable lifestyle was either a taboo or simply inaccessible for those who were willing. She is a person who has seen her own personal evolution and is now setting a benchmark of quality for many to follow.

For the latest happenings in the world of stylish accessorizing, visit www.stylefiesta.com.

Rachana Nagranee *kick started* **Pitaraa** *with the motto of making Handcrafted Happiness available to one and all in the form of bags and other fashion accessories.*

Business of Happiness

Rachana Nagranee

In a quiet house in the royal city of Nawabs – Lucknow, resided a free soul with dreams of spreading happiness and creating something with joy and style. The idea was to kindle smiles on people's faces, inspire joy around, and in doing so, to connect with their inner creative side. From that one idea in her mind and enthusiasm in her sprawl, Rachana has come a long way ahead, taking her dream forward along with the charm and delicacy of what one may call a seven course succulent meal of fashion, served perfectly to the liking and flavour of each seeker. Having found the most desired outlet for her professional and personal aspirations, Rachana Nagranee is now a proud owner of not only a fashion statement that has a huge fan following, but also a brand that is known for its personal touch and affectionate understanding of its users – a perfect blend of fashionable happiness.

Delighting its customers for about five years now, Pitaraa – signifying its real ethos of being a chest full of happiness – is a range of fashion solutions that is built to cater to the needs of its customers with an array of fashion products. Their range includes a collection starting from clutches and tote bags to jewellery and accessories of the latest styles. Apart from that, they present exclusive range of accessories and a jewellery collection dedicated specially to work outfits. Despite being a NIFT (National Institute of Fashion Technology) graduate in fashion design, which is a popular and well-sought placement position by most of the top fashion brands of the country, Rachana has taken the road less travelled to reach the stage of her vocational conquest where she stands looking back at the challenges she has met along the way to be here. "It wasn't easy to refuse a gigantic corporate package, especially when the air of success in my times was strictly measured by the weight of the pay cheque," reflects Rachana. Notwithstanding the challenge and pressure that she faced against the common trend, Rachana had made up her mind to do something of her own and not give in to the flow of convenience. Standing by her opinion to create something independently, with the purpose of providing an elevating experience to anyone who wants fashion elucidations, she continued to explore the possibilities in search for her true calling. Eventually she moved to Bangalore, with chances of finding better leads to meeting the objective of her life. This one decision, in retrospection, brought the enthusiasm, opportunity and freedom for the young entrepreneur to make life changing choices – ones that later helped her evolve both professionally as well as personally.

Recollecting the stepping stones that helped her to progress from dreams to actionable accounts, she talks about the contributions and support that helped change her thoughts into reality. "The most influencing trigger in the course of this professional exploration came through my husband," shares Rachana, "when he gifted me a singer sewing machine as his mark of support and encouragement."

Excited and geared up to make the best of this opportunity, she bagged the chance to platform her skills and creativity, quite literally! With passion in her heart and talent in her hands, Rachana worked on her first independent project. Her first designed bag was stitched and ready in a week! While working diligently at it out of sheer interest, little had the sincere Rachana known back then that the first threads into the fabric, made from her love, affection and excitement, would lead to the birth of the magnificent Pitaraa.

"I knew it, from that very moment that I have found the direction I have been looking for all this while. The joy of creating something, being involved with it so personally, and most importantly, being able to share it with people who enjoy and desire for something magical was all that I needed to start working with the idea," gleams an excited Rachana.

Pitaraa, that began with its roots defined in its motto as 'handcrafted happiness', reflects truthfully on the spirits of its creator and creations. Signaturing typically with its unique style and spectacular designs of colour palettes, with an Indianized touch to fabrics and prints, the products offer an experience which is exclusive – right from the choice of style to the final delivery of the choice.

"The pleasure of watching someone opening a 'pitaraa' and feeling the same affection and flavour that has gone into designing the product is exactly what we have to offer in the form of a box full of happiness," explains Rachana with a resonance of the ethos of the brand. She understands and appreciates the Indian sense of fashion in a way that is unique in the immensely westernized product trend around. Believing in the uniqueness of ethnicity and its strong connection with the consumers of the nation, Rachana dedicates her collection to the texture of a style that is indigenous to the Indian soil. That explains not only the exclusivity of the products, but also the appreciation she finds across customers of all ages. Defining happiness with something as fundamental as "black coffee, a small garden and an adorable cat", Rachana believes in montaging the conventional with the bold. In her creations, she has combined the experience of fashion with the celebratory leisure for both Pitaraa as well as its users. Knowing that attention paid to the little details of what makes a product desirable and acceptable to the right set of audience has helped her build the brand identity with one that is dedicated to creating a fashion experience instead of merely a commercial transaction.

With every experience, Rachana has attempted to present her dreams at a bigger and more creative platform. With an ever-rising support from people across all verticals, Pitaraa is now recognized through both physical and virtual presence in lives of people. It now proudly stands with a following of more than 20,000 fans on Facebook. Talking about how fashion and business had begun expanding into different paths, she reveals the litmus test that got her to believe she was on the right track with her passion. "Two years ago, we had started retailing in local boutiques. We witnessed an instant acceptance...there's been no looking back since!" she expresses excitedly.

After having instilled confidence and acceptance amongst buyers in India, Pitaraa has also taken determinant steps and has made global expeditions. Stepping into the international market, Pitaraa is now spreading its wings fashionably in the US, UK, Malayasia, Singapore and Hongkong. This has not just been a step up in terms of the magnitude of the brand, but an opportunity to make an intricate experience available for customers from across the world. This steadily growing affection and acceptance across the globe is only reinstating the fact that happiness in different forms can be shared and relished by everybody, notwithstanding their geographical and cultural boundaries. Portraying contemporary style of fashion with an Indian tone of colours, patterns and textures, Pitaraa has been marking its niche amidst an international audience on both online and offline platforms.

As a mark of success, what Rachana calls a report card for her evaluation, recognition on reputed forums serves as a source of inspiration as well as a quality control incentive to meet the exemplary standards that Pitaraa has set for itself. Showcased at the Rosemount Australia Fashion Week in May 2010, Pitaraa has found representation in front of some of the most renowned names in the fashion industry, that too, at a very early stage in its operational stage. Attributing this milestone of success to the very essence that marked the value of Pitaraa, she says, "Our uniqueness lies in true happiness and elegance of the experience that purchasing a Pitaraa brings." She goes on to explain how every purchase is designed as a moment of proud ownership for its users. From choicest offerings in the range of products to delivering the product with its suave and effective packaging makes the receiver ecstatic. "This is exactly what I had set out to achieve…to spread happiness. I am happy to see I am getting somewhere," she beams contently. This principle pretty much explains her focus on the details of what the brand connects to its users. She believes in the philosophy of sharing Pitaraa as a legacy in its physical as well as metaphysical form rather than just a shiny object in a woman's hand. To her mind, this is both empowering and engaging for her users, an image she clearly believes reflects Pitaraa's identity.

To find happiness in one's passion is a blessing one may learn. But what keeps the brand running is something one may want to learn with experience. "What makes me going is practically the business," she reveals with a twinkle, but adds swiftly, "But what keeps the business going is complete faith and undying positivity. I had started Pitaraa to share the feeling and experience of happiness that I feel every time I create something and that is precisely what keeps me moving forward even in the most difficult and challenging times."

You'd wonder where this is going, what's the next step and if there's a business plan to take things forward for Pitaraa. Echoing the egalitarian spirit of happiness that she radiates, Rachana envisages to bring Pitaraa to the reach of people of all ages and tastes.

"Fashion solutions from seventeen to seventy years of age," she states confidently. She believes that happiness must not be confined within definitions of any sort. Resonating with cheerfulness and an unending wave of creative impulse, Rachana is a true reflection of the joy she kindles with her brand. Opening boxes of happiness for people around her, she is seen talking and sharing ideas with everyone with the same enthusiasm – taking feedback, exchanging smiles and offering coffee.

"I am excited to own a Pitaraa," exclaims a seventy-year-old woman with extraordinary zeal. "I can't wait to take it out and show it to my friends when we go out the next time," she shares her excitement with Rachana.

Rachana had started off with a small stitch – what may have sounded like a whim to the people who did not believe in her. But the waves of happiness it has spread across the believers and the magical happiness one can feel with a connection built with Pitaraa goes beyond a customer-brand relationship. She stands tall as an example of pursuing one's dreams, not for selfish achievements, but for the pristine joy of sharing and watching people smile. More than the ownership of a commodity, it is a phenomenon that is outshining its own position in a capitalistically inclined arena where emotions speak a hundred times louder than purchase orders. Such enterprises are born with aspirations of creating ripples of relations and emotions more than simply adding to the online clutter of commercial exchange. They stand as symbolic inspiration to people with dreams, and with ideas that are out of the box. Despite challenges and risks, Rachana has made her niche in a space of commerce with the sheer drive force of her passion for creativity and faith in her goodwill for people. A true example of a life that would motivate people to dream and follow their own paths, Pitaraa is a collection of pride, fashion and expression of true happiness.

Handcrafted bags and fashion accessories are just a click away at www.pitaraa.com.

Richa Kar *founded* **Zivame** *– an online lingerie retailer – with a vision to change the entire convention and experience of lingerie shopping for Indian women.*

What Shines Underneath?

Richa Kar

Sometimes it takes an opportunity to change your perspective towards life. Sometimes it takes a deep insight and sometimes a lot of experience before you can dive head long into creating a beginning. When all the three combine, however, it is most likely that a masterpiece is produced. One that exemplifies skill, perseverance and intelligence mechanized into a body. Now whether this chances to be a personal development, a philosophical quest or quite visibly an entrepreneurial climb, the results are extraordinary. One such enterprise that has risen out of nowhere in the last four years has broken predictable boundaries, both of its success as well as nature. Redefining conventions, generating an entirely new consumer segment and habit, the inspirational e-commerce portal has caught the eye of brands, users and the media alike.

Richa Kar, a qualified engineer from one of the best institutes of the country had it in her to combine her skills with her opportunities and change things around for her and thousands of women across the country. After completing her MBA, Richa did what most in her generation would do. She was placed in one of the coveted IT stalwarts of the country and delved into various segments of retailing, branding and operations. During this course, she worked with many different channels of marketing and held a position as a consultant to global retailers. However, unlike many others who can safely fall into this genre of bright marketing experts, this retailer at heart found the courage and acumen to take it to the next level.

"I always knew I had to build something of my own. And I had clearly realized through my experience that if I did build something, it would have to do with the end consumers. All I was waiting for was to find that one alarming problem that could be solved by a great idea," she speaks recollecting the days of initiation. As a keen observer and interpreter of market strengths and opportunities, she was always open to learning about different sectors. It was this eagerness to learn and her encounter as a consultant to a global lingerie brand that it occurred to Richa that this was an industry waiting to be explored and ploughed in the right fashion. "In India, the lingerie segment is so under-served! There is a dearth of appropriate information, sizes and styles. Also, in India, the category is filled with taboos and misconceptions making it all the more challenging."

Richa goes on to talk about the taboo, including openly shopping for lingerie which has reduced the essential commodity into a five minute hurried purchase from male-dominated stores. This is when the insightful retailer froze her choice of enterprise in the segment of lingerie and decided then to change the entire convention and experience of lingerie shopping for Indian women. This led to the foundation of a brand that has today become the largest selling lingerie platform of the country and is bookmarked as a favourite amidst women across ages and backgrounds. In the year 2011, this e-commerce platform was launched by the attractive name of Zivame.

The fascinating name is more than just an attractive sound; it reflects the ethos of the brand very appropriately. Derived from Hebrew, the name translates to 'radiant me'.

"I wanted to create a place for women where they would be free to embrace their bodies and build their confidence; a place where her intimate necessity does not make her feel judged and disrespected, but rather makes her feel liberated and celebrated."

It is with this objective that Richa chose the online platform as opposed to retail stores. "It's more private, consultative and comfortable too!" she adds promptly. Instead of just 'selling' a product, Zivame aims to educate its customers about the category so that they make informed choices. The brand also follows the concept of 'discreet packaging' so that customers do not feel uneasy when they receive their order in any environment. Overall, the brand offers her an experience that is both liberating and exciting.

Does a platform like online shopping work for something as personal as lingerie, one may wonder. But Zivame and Richa have demonstrated just that. A big fan of online shopping herself, she speaks about how time and cost effective the platform is and at the same time provides such efficiency of range, comparatives and privacy. "That's the best possible recipe for lingerie shopping," she adds with a laugh.

Breaking the apprehensive myth for women across India, Zivame makes an ingenious portal that allows for size charts, reference of fitting through images and an extremely user friendly return policy. Taking the experience a step further, Richa has even opened a fitting lounge in Bangalore that allows customers to come and interact with fitting experts and discover their right fit. "I can understand what my end consumers need, because I am them! That makes for a key strength for us," she talks with an understanding of her target audience. In the beginning of the enterprise, Richa recalls she used to receive calls from users and would use the pseudonym Sindu and try to understand their buying pattern, likes and dislikes and areas of problems. It was this in-depth involvement in her business and such direct connection with her consumers that brought her to the level of their understanding and experience. It is not surprising then that all strategies designed and employed by the dynamic entrepreneur have hit home with women across the country, irrespective of their tastes, styles, ages or social set-up. Recollecting one of the initial experiences, Richa talks about a to-be bride who had injured her leg and couldn't shop for her wedding and honeymoon. "We helped her identify her body type and size. She was really excited when she had the lingerie delivered at her doorstep." When experiences like this started occurring more often, Richa was certain that she was on the right track!

The heights the extraordinary brand has achieved in the last few years are hard to ignore. But there have been numerous challenges and hurdles that go unnoticed amidst the charm and optimism of the astounding founder. "When my mother first got to know that her daughter was getting into a business of selling lingerie, she was shocked!" Richa exclaims. This was also a hurdle that she had to face in the other dimensions of her enterprise building. Just talking about lingerie was difficult. To break those social boundaries, to convince people to come on board and to have women believe that this was an experience worth making for themselves was foremost. Furthermore, the set-up for Zivame in itself was a challenge. From finding an appropriate office space to hiring an efficient team, from acquiring safe payment gateways to partnering up with the best brands, Richa persevered through the whole process boisterously. However, the hard work did pay off. Having put together a team that she is fond and proud of, Richa looks back at the days of struggle with a sense of achievement. It is with this optimism that her venture now sports over five thousand styles of lingerie to choose from, all accepted, appreciated and endorsed by her many thousands of satisfied customers.

Taking pride in the uniqueness of Zivame, she talks about the brand's dedication to keeping their customers happy and satisfied at all stages of the retailer-buyer experience. Speaking fondly of her customer service, Richa explains how an entire dedicated team focuses on the user experience. From creating more user interactive interface online, to training their telecom points of contact for the customers, quality is of prime importance for her. One reason why Zivame can be credited to retaining its customers and receiving a ginormous amount of referrals is because of the user experience it creates.

"We had a customer call in who was planning a weekend getaway to Goa; she didn't have time but needed something exciting. We were able to help her identify her body-type and the kind of shapewear and swimwear she could wear. Later, she wrote to us saying she loved the stuff we sent her and that she looks great in all her pictures!" What gets the entrepreneur to hit the bull's eye each time is using the insight of her customer and not merely thinking like a business woman who has set out to make a profit. "Every time we set out to try something new, or are in the process of launching a new feature, or collection, I always put myself in the shoes of my buyers. I know that if I get this element right, business will flow by itself."

Keeping the customer first not only is her policy but her mantra for success, and Richa has crossed many milestones in the significant journey of her path-breaking entrepreneurship. Yet, humbly marking each achievement as a progress made by the women of the country, she speaks fondly of the change that has come about in the experience of lingerie shopping for women.

Zivame has been the first online shopping experience for about 20% of women in the country. The age old trend of mothers buying lingerie for their daughters till they get married has also seen a major shift. Today girls and women of different profiles have started understanding and experimenting with their requirements and tastes in lingerie. Marking this as a sign of revolution and evolution, Richa agrees that Zivame is heading closer to its aspiration and ethos.

Working hard towards perfection and giving credit where it's due are the attributes that have made Richa a favourite amidst her young and energetic team. With the ambition of 'creating magic, one lingerie box at a time', the dedicated team works together with harmony and creativity, both assets encouraged tremendously by their robust CEO. With a promising career growth and a learning experience in e-commerce, Zivame is fast becoming a desired destination for many young aspiring entrepreneurs. Their current strength has crossed the whooping number of two hundred happy members. Creating an efficiently professional environment, and yet keeping the energy high with creativity, typical Zivame energy is maintained with enthusiastic table tennis matches, reverbing music, both recorded and live, as well as a food for thought as well as the tummy in abundance for the members to recharge. This, however, is followed by a signature 'lingerie knowledge test' for each new employee, setting benchmarks for internalizing the sentiment of the brand they are working for.

What started as a singular ambition in a one-bedroom apartment, in the head of an engineer and marketing expert, took shape into creating a revolutionary experience for what today tolls to about three lakh women behind their computer screens. If numbers are to be analysed, Zivame today sells more than one bra per minute, amounting to more than 1440 lingerie pieces in a day!

The brand has found several repeated mentions amidst the top ranking fashion magazines, business channels, both on and offline. As a woman who encourages the physical mark of womanhood to be cherished and celebrated, Richa has broken many conventions, raised many eyebrows and yet found an overwhelming liking and support across the country. With Richa at the helm, the glass ceiling just doesn't exist at Zivame. Also, while one may tend to assume that women will form the majority of the workforce with Zivame being a lingerie company, the organization comes across as extremely diverse with the workforce consisting of equal number of men and women. With her own definition for business, style and consumerism, Richa stands as an inspiration for many aspiring women to follow. In her work, as well as her belief, she resonates with strength and determination that can dismiss all apprehensions, constraints and reservations that may fall in one's path towards actualizing one's dreams. Richa is, in real sense, an embodiment of radiance.

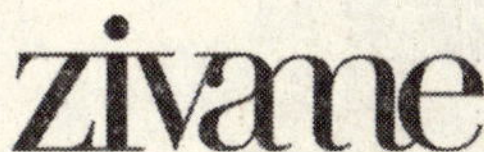

www.zivame.com is a premier online lingerie store, providing one platform to all leading national and international brands.

Sneha Raisoni, *fondly known as Tappu, opened her very own shop* **Tappu ki Dukaan** *to exhibit objects that are quirky, unique and fun in their appearance and utility.*

A Store Full of Fun

Sneha Raisoni

When a top shot employee of a premium investment banking unit quits her job and walks out of her stable career of more than five years, you can either be shocked at the unpredictability of such a drastic step, or prepare yourself to witness the beginning of something extraordinary. In the lives of most people, the comforts of the predictable, the stable or the normal take precedence over anything that may sound remotely risky, but there are a few daring souls, who believe in challenging the norms, in stepping away from conventions and making a routine of the extraordinary way of life. When such people step out of their comfort zones to pursue the unpredictable, it reflects strongly on their passion and dedication, making stories that inspire many others.

Sneha Raisoni is an exemplary entrepreneur who has crossed boundaries of a conventional career and built her own space, quite literally. A vocationally qualified chartered accountant by conformist definitions, the accounts expert had been working stably in a renowned investment banking organization for five years before realizing she needed to do something on her own.

"It was a series of events that brought me to the realization that I needed to get out and pursue my own passion instead of someone else's dreams."

An argument with the ex-boss, and an empty space waiting to be explored were all just minor triggers to the transformation that had been building up in her consciousness. The real motivation was born out of Sneha's desperate wish to develop her own free space to work and express. Her creative inclination, having lay dormant for all these years, yearned for expression and exploration. While the external circumstances pushed her further away from the monotony of a patterned life, her internal turmoil was preparing her for the makeover her life was about to adopt. And one day, just like that, the aspiring explorer quit her job and set out to build her outlet of creativity in both the metaphorical and literal sense! What began as a journey to express her creative mettle transpired into a structure that stands today as a symbol of her radical and innovative venture, Tappu ki Dukaan.

In the posh locality of the fort area in Mumbai, where routine and normalcy echoes in every structure and habit, Tappu ki Dukaaan is a bustling nest of creative exhibition. It is a store that feeds your imagination, and has objects that are quirky, unique and fun in their appearance and utility.

"I have been in this area for quite some time now and I came to realize that though the suburbs of Mumbai have stores that exhibit creative products, the town area had no such outlets, and if there were any, they were so expensive that one would think twice before entering one." Explaining the market opportunity and its amalgamation with Sneha's desire to create a space for her own expression, she decided to set up a name that brings together the wackiest, most creative and unique products from the most fun and expressive brands of the country. These include products ranging from Happily Unmarried to Mukul Goyal, Haathi Chhap, Pop goes the Art, Mixed Juice, etc.

"In Tappu Ki Dukaan, you don't get things that you merely need; it's a place where you'll find things that captivate your attention enough to make you want to own it," she explains in excitement.

Fondly known as TeekDee, Sneha's brain child offers anything from ash trays shaped like commodes, shot glasses, playing cards, cushions, bookmarks made of cow dung, etc. Basically it's a buffet of humour, creativity and style, all mixed in packs of fun and ingenious products. Strategically and reasonably priced between rupees forty and four thousand, the store offers fun in affordable prices.

"The idea is to inspire and encourage creative exploration, to break the monotony of people's routine taste and lifestyle, but without burning a hole in their pockets", she adds insightfully. Putting herself in the place of her customers, Sneha visualizes their tastes, will of expenditure and evolving notion of fun, and creates her display of products accordingly. Her solemn attempt to add fun and flavour in the lives of people around her has brought the young entrepreneur recognition and acceptance in a way that motivates her towards exploring new width of success.

Recollecting the genesis of Tappu Ki Dukaan, Sneha reveals the character she poured into the brand. The quirky, fun-loving and light-spirited soul that she is, Sneha believes in the reflection of the same in her life, her work and in general, the energy she radiates around herself. Finding contentment in the little joys and celebrating a creative expression in life, she believes Tappu Ki Dukaan is a true embodiment of herself. Even before the store actually came out in its physical form, Sneha knew that it was her own fun-filled and creative energy that was resonating in its idea all along. Sneha talks about strengthening her will and wisdom with all the lessons that the start-up taught her. Every need and necessity was looked after once the determination of this quirky spot had taken shape. Blessed with goodwill and friends who support her through thick and thin, she got together her savings and finance from a good friend to get the dice rolling for her venture. Eventually, Tappu Ki Dukaan came to be in the free space Sneha had at hand, and set out in business. There has been no looking back since then, only a fun and creative journey for the CA turned entrepreneur.

With an ambience that reflects both the motivation as well as the nature of the store, Tappu Ki Dukaan is designed imaginatively and attractively for its customers. Walls sporting a mural of a spider web spun around, creatively dangling photo frames across the web, colours and presentation all sprinkled with the theme of fun and entertainment, encourage customers to spend plenty of time in the store and enjoy the experience of creativity rather than just engage in a commercial transaction.

"My mantra is utility with a twist," she adds with a spark, "and I want the whole experience to invoke people to try fun and innovative things in life. Whether it is a five-year-old kid or a fifty-year-old man, we all need to keep our creative side alive," she reflects the ethos of Tappu Ki Dukaan.

Catering to the tastes of young students, middle-aged professionals or housewives seeking something creative for their homes, the out of the box space is now an accepted trend-setter with several loyal fans and customers in south Mumbai.

Speaking of the business model, Sneha shares the simple cycle behind the complicated layers of homework she has done to bring together her enterprise. After long periods of perseverance with different brands, she has managed to bring together the best collection of products catering to tastes and affordability of her target audience. "I source from various designers across the country and retail through my store…some are on consignment and some I purchase outright," she explains.

Aspiring to take her creative expression to the next level, the dynamic one woman army wishes to build her own line of creative products. Envisaging her own range of manufactured quirky objects of utility, she also plans to expand her Tappu Ki Dukaan to other parts of the country to spread the same spirit of fun-filled experience of creative enterprise.

As a patron of creative inspiration, Sneha believes in work rather than names. Currently working with brands that were once themselves start-ups known for their breakthrough pioneering in respective streams of products, she endorses innovation and risk-taking, both in business as well as in creativity. Welcoming new designers, thinkers and creators who dare to break the convention and create something out of the box, she expresses her respect and appreciation for everyone who is an artist.

"My store is a platform for design…all those youngsters and people who are gifted with talent to create something (and sometimes, something out of nothing) can easily approach me and showcase their products through my store," she smiles emphatically. Stressing on the importance of accessibility, especially for new designers, she reveals the process of collaboration with Tappu Ki Dukaan as one being simple, transparent and time-efficient. Keeping the terms and conditions to the minimal, Sneha accentuates the need for the product to be creative and quirky as the only criteria to be accepted in the fun house.

With time, Tappu ki Dukaan has found recognition not only in its neighbourhood and word of mouth benefaction, but the store has also witnessed its share of appreciation as it finds mention in newspaper articles, magazines, websites and news channels through which the popularity of this hub of fun has multiplied. The young entrepreneur, who is content with where life has taken her, firmly believes in building relationships with her customers to flourish in the long term. From making user experience in the store as unique and friendly, to providing home delivery options, from options of ordering online to availability of customization, the user experience of Tappu Ki Dukaan is what attracts people as much as the products themselves. "I am not a very ambitious entrepreneur," she explains, "which is why I am not easily threatened by competition. I guess that in itself works in my favour as a latent strength." With rising popularity comes the blatant replication of the model in the neighbourhood. While this may result in risks of secretive collaboration with product suppliers, an achievement Sneha had earned after a great deal of hard work, for the stark optimist, such instances only create opportunities for her to evolve and continue striving for more imagination, more innovation. This is a challenge she is happy to embrace! An extension of this spirit is seen in her latest venture, Roti, Kapda aur Makaan, a sister outlet, just as whacky as its name sounds. The café cum décor hub is another of her expressions of out of the box products. The added feature of having a café along with the shopping store gives people more time to be a part of the fun ambience, even engage their little ones in fun activities like doodling on quirky boards. Taking her creativity a couple of notches higher than the regular, Sneha endorses the idea of living in a fun and quirky manner.

Looking back at her days of a stable job and predictable routines, Sneha shrugs with a confirmative no when asked if she misses any of that. Extremely happy and content with the risks she has taken and roads she has walked, she stands today as a proud owner of a flourishing enterprise, a battle she has fought single-handedly. With due appreciation to her friends and family for their unending support and confidence in her, Sneha smiles at the prospect of one or the other creative bubble that keep popping in her head through the day. "When someone walks into the store and says something like 'Hey, this is exactly what I wanted!', I know I am doing the right thing." Her smile glints with satisfaction.

"People come here, experience happiness, take a part of this joy with them, and even go on to share and gift it to the others, that's all I have ever wanted."

Not only as a business hub, Tappu ki Dukaan, today stands as a gift on metaphorical level too. As an offering to people bringing a breath of fresh air, the enterprise is exemplary for today's aspiring entrepreneurs to take the leap of faith, for themselves, as well as for the others to participate in.

Visit www.tappukidukaan.com or the real store for some fun, quirky merchandise for you and yours.

Sunita Jaju *(left) and* **Swati Maheshwari** *are environment enthusiasts who got together to launch* **Rustic Art** *- a portal creating and selling eco-friendly and organic products of everyday utility.*

Nurture of Nature

Swati Maheshwari and Sunita Jaju

A small, inconspicuous corner in the college campus somewhere in India is bustling with excitement. A group of enthusiasts are staring through their lenses into what they imagine will be the future of a healthier, greener way of life. Somewhere amidst this frolic of friends and well-wishers is a nervous Swati, watching her aspirations finally taking form in these humble beginnings. The Kanpur-born communication specialist, Swati Maheshwari has come a long way from determining a career into moulding what can be seen as a sustainable way of life with organic and environment-friendly products of everyday life. Having been nourished by the generous arms of nature in the lush valley of Nainital in the north of India, Swati has grown to value the fast-depleting serenity of pure nature amidst human habitat. To bring back the pristine and natural into common everyday lifestyle, she strives with her passion and profession to make footprints for a healthier world. In this endeavour, she finds vehement backing of her near and dear ones.

Living in the lap of the serene hills of Mysore, Sunita has always been nature's child. An environmentalist by passion and entrepreneur by profession, she has walked the roads to promote an eco-friendly regime. In subtle ways of living, or altering lifestyles altogether, she believes in the necessity of harmony with nature. The exorbitant use of chemicals in the eco-system bothers her enough to take an intolerant stand against it – to the extent for her to form an organization that is taking one step at a time to offer an ecological solution of healthy living.

When the paths of the two environment enthusiasts cross as friends, relatives and well-wishers, they know something needs to be made of this conglomeration. Despite having no experience in enterprise building, Swati and Sunita find motivation in their passion to create organic alternatives to the chemical obsession. Pushing their limits, the women partnered to take up the brave challenge of what has now known to become Rustic Art, an effort to create organic life with a range of personal, health, child care and laundry products that are eco-friendly, in both composition and usage. The laundry range, for example, is a hundred percent non-toxic and hence, the water from the washing machines is still environment friendly and can be used to water plants.

"Our products are pollution free. Even in our packaging, we try to keep waste to a minimum and promote eco-friendly substances. We want our love for the environment to reflect in every step of our actions; that's how we feel about Rustic Art," reveals Swati with deep commitment. How love for nature has transpired into an enterprise is a revelation of an important journey by the two think tanks of Rustic Art.

"Our greatest support has come from within the circle of family and friends – people who matter the most," she explains meaningfully. Believing that the strongest influences and changes begin at home, the two partners started with distributing samples to their near and dear ones to estimate the response. Finding motivation in the positive feedback, they moved ahead with handing out free samples at nearby stores.

Admitting to the hiccups during the initial testing of the products, Swati also acknowledges that while the sale responses hadn't been up to the mark, the products had been unanimously accepted and appreciated. "This was a sign for us to tread ahead better equipped to address the market," she admits sincerely. With better assessment and experience the second time, Rustic Art reemerged in the online marketing section for its selective audience. Donned with branding designed by a dear friend, and systemized with the support of well-wishers, it wasn't difficult for the two novices to see that no other brand offered the quality in the price bracket that Rustic Art was offering to its consumers. "Soon we had repeat orders. And since then, there's been no looking back," Swati reminisces with contentment.

Having introduced a wide range of products from personal to child care and even a charming addition of pet care, Swati and Sunita, related through family as well as through their fervour for the environment, have ironed out many hurdles in the last four years. With no former conventional experience or education in business development, the duo brought in their passion to the avocation with their background of communication and sustainable development as mapping tools of progress. Recollecting the challenges that mushroomed in the initial phase, Swati talks about her struggles of juggling between strenuous college years and a demanding business stake. Being in different cities and scuttling to build networks didn't help the partners during the starting stage. But overcoming the challenges with sheer determination, these nature lovers have been rising higher year after year. In a largely male-dominated business arena, the pair feels absolutely secure and admits to enjoy the attention and support they get from family members and friends alike.

"I think it's extremely essential to believe in your product before you can sell it to the market. In addition, to be an entrepreneur, you need to have passion for your field of venture. Otherwise it's just impossible to sustain," reflects Swati on what has kept Rustic Arts growing sustainably over the years.

True to their spirit of harmonious existence with nature, the commercial approach for Rustic Arts also resonates their deep commitment to promoting a healthy environment and appreciating any other 'competitor' in the vertical who helps to spread the 'green' message with intensions of coexisting with brands of similar ideologies. What makes them stand out, the onlookers wonder? It is the personal and honest involvement that both Swati and Sunita have devoted to Rustic Arts. "It's just the two of us taking things together, with a few members to help us with the stocks and office," they say. Devoting a considerable amount of time and resources into the message that echoes through the brand, they believe that it is important for people to understand the force behind the products. The packaging of each and every product of Rustic Art includes a key message that helps to create an understanding and awareness about not only the origin and specialty of the products, but also voices an appeal to adopting an organic way of life. The true witness of this growing wave is not in the expanding numbers of sales but in the feedback and support Rustic Art builds with each connection. "It feels wonderful to see people understanding and conceding to the ideology we have built Rustic Art around. When on international forums like Menope in Dubai (2011) we got to voice this movement, we knew there's hope and support for the cause we are working on," gleams Swati.

A prism of symbiosis arrays at Rustic Art with friends and associates all helping out like a family. Functioning with mettle of more than running a business, Swati has been buoyant in both professional and personal fronts, "just like Rustic Art that believes in the balance of natural existence," she explains vibrantly. Offering to deliver only the best, Swati, along with her aunt and partner Sunita, has been striving to magnify the reach of the products democratically. They envisage building production units locally in Maharashtra in the near future.

Amidst the hustle and bustle of a delivery day, Swati remembers a funny incident. She talks about a family member who had been using a Rustic Art bathing soap for a while and realized that her skin was glowing exceptionally. She was asked which soap she was using. It was mirthful to discover that she had been using our laundry soap as a bathing soap! The family had a good laugh but it was noticeable that since the laundry soap is made with natural ingredients, it only helped to remove tan and caused no harm to the skin at all! Recollecting what had been an amusing instance in the family, Swati walks away to attend to the needs of the staff, leaving one to wonder at the honest generosity of nature that brings no harm in its offering and is in the urgent need of reprisal through efforts like Rustic Art to win the battle against pollution, deforestation and the like.

Alicia Souza *is a born artist and skilled illustrator, with many brand names like Google, Yahoo, Penguin, Cadbury, AOL and others on her list of acquired clients.*

The Art of Life

Alicia Souza

A peek into her usual morning routine – two cups of coffee and jostling through her two pooches, she kick starts her day with a new spring of delight, and rushes head on, bursting with creative challenges. With a lively, spirited attitude, Alicia Souza is one of the most conspicuously rising stars in the arena of professional illustration in India. Happy, curious, full of words and exciting stories – the description fits her just as precisely as her illustrations. Freelancer by choice and free spirited by heart, Alicia runs her own enterprise from her vibrant studio in the city of Bangalore in India and spreads her ideas across the world through colourful illustrations.

Having lived a major part of her live in the Middle East, Alicia has had the opportunity to move around in different continents. Not more than five years ago, she decided to move to her current location where the young and chirpy illustrator has been freelancing with the big names in the country, marking the beginning of her 'real' career. She holds a degree in communication design and conforms to her pledge of illustrating only for the design field after her first job. Recalling the initial incidents that led her into the field of designing she reveals:

"I was away from the city when a local Melbourne newspaper had come to review the students' folios for illustration. It was only through my teacher's mail that I got to know that she wanted to commission me as an illustrator. And that was it. My first steps into illustrating began from thereon!" Having chanced into being a freelance artist, Alicia, however, did not just stumble into her art by chance. Recalling her first work of art at the age of three, she even blogs about a drawing of a scooter on a door with only chalk as her fond memory. It was therefore nothing of a surprise when her polished skills as an illustrator brought her into the big books of art at a rather young age. The artist already has many brand names like Google, Yahoo, Penguin, Cadbury, AOL and others on her list of acquired clients, despite being a fairly new name in the Indian region.

She doesn't deny having come this far without her share of hurdles and troubles. "Everything about starting out was hard. The fact that I hardly knew anyone, and India was still relatively new to me and just getting used to the dailies of freelancing life was not all that easy for me," she says. Having sustained from the waves of a staggering start that most of the self-made enterprises sink in, she now makes light of the initial nervous moments where she would give herself pep-talks before client meetings. Being her own mentor, she had to find her own way into becoming a professional.

Working for herself turned out to be an accidental blessing. "I hadn't planned on being a freelancer. I just happened to stumble into it through a series of events and I gathered I liked it after all!" exclaims the bright-eyed entrepreneur. Alicia stoically credits the success of the unremitting path of a freelance career to her diligence, discipline and love for her work. Despite the sincere undertones, she does however admit that working from her comfortable spot in her pyjamas is the greatest perk of being her own boss!

The youthful illustrator who has an absorbent attitude towards her ambience, talks about everything that has impacted her life in ways big and small. She holds this very strength responsible for making her what she is. Moments as heart wrenching as the death of her beloved dog Cookie Brown, or as exciting as her first live show amidst an audience, all come into the list of the 'manys' that have affected, inspired and helped her evolve as a being both in her personal and professional climb.

"I still remember the time I was first exposed to an artwork that made me watch and melt into it," she reminisces about her first experience with the work of Quinten Blake who has been an important influence for her many expressions. In her own fashion of finding art in everyday life, she explains that her source of inspiration comes from anywhere and everything around her. However, it is worth a thought to remember that heading in the direction of becoming an illustrator did not win her the same confidence from the outside world as it did from her inner conviction. Describing the first reaction from her family, Alicia goes on to explain how the idea of making a stable living out of her drawings was a little too hard to digest for her parents. However, the 'show and tell' attitude of this go-getter only strengthened their faith in her over time as her career took a more stable track and found her more recognition and success than they would have initially fathomed.

"I am glad they did not lecture me or try to talk me out of my choice. I can't thank them enough for letting me figure things out on my own," she declares in retrospect. Accrediting her most impactful teacher to life itself, the thoughtful woman testifies that real learning comes with experience out in the real world. "Maybe I did not learn all that much in the classrooms. But when I was a student, I learnt about myself, about things I didn't like, and about the importance of how to be schedule and research well," she adds fondly.

Being the boss of her enterprise as well as her life choices, Alicia shares about her love for her two pet dogs, her passion for drawing, cooking, fixing things and doing the laundry with just about as much enthusiasm as her work. She is a yoga enthusiast and believes in bringing about diversity in her world in and outside of work. Having her mind and heart immersed in the art, she accepts that she clearly wouldn't have been happy if she weren't doing what she does for her loving and living.

"I have no regrets about where I am and even if I were given a chance to go back and change something about this journey, I would pass!" she says with pride. As someone who respects her professional approach towards work and its discipline, Alicia talks about loving the space she shares with contemporary artists.

"They help to make this industry better and bigger. I don't take them as competitors." Explaining every project as a new and exciting experience, the coffee fan keeps at her toes with finding a challenge in each of her assignments. "I like doing things that don't make me too comfortable so that I can keep growing at all times," she says illuminating her secret mantra to a positive and progressive take on life and work.

With resonance of her inner creativity in both actions and attitude, Alicia believes in sharing the knowledge and experience of creativity with anyone who would like to learn sincerely. The Top Illustrating Student Award winner spares time travelling in the country to deliver TEDx talks in various colleges on the subject of creativity. Inspiring many pioneering artists, she has been a source of direction for them to pursue the unconventional career path of becoming an illustrator.

"I advise them to be diligent and hardworking," she puts the ingredients to her success simplistically. Sending out a word to both boys and girls aspiring to become artists or start their enterprises, she encourages them to pursue her dream with sincerity and discipline – assets that came naturally to her and helped her hold strong during the challenges of grounding her feet in India at the early age of twenty-two. Never having let being a woman stop her in any way to become an entrepreneur in India, Alicia confesses to the challenges of starting out without a mentor.

"Stay strong while watching out for the vendors that make dealing a nightmare", she adds jokingly.

One would think that to travel around the world, station oneself in a world created with the impression of art and joy of mugs full of coffee and with loving dogs on one's lap would be a farce many would dismiss as a dream. Some would say it is a path not worth the risk. Who likes to trade with convention after all? Some others would argue against the fate of an independent start-up living in a country that lies out of comfort zone. But Alicia Souza cannot be counted into the list of many. Having taken her childhood scribbles up as the one passion that she has realized into reality, she stands to defy all notions of what we have labelled as impossible. Not only does she stand tall as an illustrator, shining brightly with her will and work, but also sets an example for many silent aspirations to look upon and find courage to follow. She is someone who lives her life to the fullest and reflects her love industriously in her work with the honesty and diligence one rarely finds in the most conventional paths of mass career choices. Alicia has demonstrated that pushing boundaries comes with more contentment than cost. With her ever-rising popularity that precedes her work in the professional sphere and steadily expanding Zen in her inner space, she reflects strongly a life worth learning and following.

Looking for quirky illustrations for your products, or want some funky merchandise to choose from, she is the woman who can help you. Visit www.aliciasouza.com for more.

Starting off as an entrepreneur in the software solutions domain, **Anisha Singh** *founded* **Mydala.com***, an easy way to indulge, save and shop.*

The E-market Mantra

Anisha Singh

Her morning starts early – rising up to get her daughters out of bed, rushing them to get ready for school, preparing for their day, and juggling chores. All this while racing against time. Kissing her angels goodbye, Anisha turns around and fixes her attention to her other, much larger family that awaits her attention for the rest of the day. Focus, strength and spontaneity get this ambitious mother of two marching through each day. Little had she imagined it would be thus, when she had moved to the United States almost two decades ago to pursue her higher education.

She hails from a typical joint family from Delhi, growing up with an army of cousins.

"Even as a child, I was a rebel without a cause, someone who knew she had to do things differently, the nonconventional way." Moving to the States for what would eventually turn into a twelve-year-long educational and experiential life turner, Anisha pursued her graduation without a strong sense of ambition or a clear direction in her head about where she was headed. It can easily be mistaken that destiny alone had a deeper implication and insistence from the ambience that then converted Anisha into believing into much more than a single-tracked persuasion of her learning.

"A professor in my university had a lot of faith in me," explains Anisha recollecting the days of when it all started. "He paid special attention to my line of thought, encouraged me to participate and engage in experiences and learning both in and outside of college. It was because of him that I decided to pursue a Master's degree in Business Administration."

This decision, followed by a flow of events, changed Anisha's perspectives towards life, allowing her to think of the scope of growth she had as a woman in the world of enterprise.

The beginning of what would become many of Anisha's entrepreneurial engagements began with her role in association with the Clinton Administration. Her primary tasks included helping women entrepreneurs raise funding for innovative women-led businesses. This turned out to be a blessing in more than one ways for her, "I was suddenly submerged into this world of dynamic women who had built their own enterprises. There were single mothers managing growing kids and expanding business, there were women fighting with minimal resources in a world dominated by men, so it was an eye-opener for me," she exclaims with appreciation in her voice. It was then that the first initial steps into the world of business brought her into facilitating the set-up of e-learning ecosystems for Fortune 500 companies. This, marking a beginning of involved and evolved ventures, led her to explore and understand the evolved space of ecommerce in America.

Having decided never to settle in a comfort zone, Anisha then moved home to India with a vision to start from ground zero and put her passion and learning about the business world into good use.

"I realized there was a lot of scope to tap the web market through India. It was then that I set up my first company, Kinis

(Software) Solutions, which till date provides customized e-learning solutions for Fortune 500 companies – a name she had been associated with even while working in the United States. Not only was this an opportunity to dive headlong into engaging with the web marketing space, but also an opportunity to build her networking in the Indian context, an avenue that she had not explored before.

It was however, the entrepreneurial bug that pushed Anisha to keep going even after having set up a flourishing and stabilized business.

"I woke up one day to realize that Kinis did not need all of my attention and time anymore. I knew then that it was time to explore, to find something new and cutting edge." Exploration got her to stumble into the collective business model of the Chinese. "It was interesting to observe how they got together on a platform to avail discounts. The same pattern also seemed to be evolving in the US. So I thought this must definitely be tried out in India." In her thorough research, Anisha had found that the surface of hybrid models of ecommerce had barely been scratched in the India scenario, the utmost being in the travel industry. It was time, she understood, to tap into the 'buy online, experience offline' mode of marketing that beckoned the Indian market.

"That's what led to the establishment of my second enterprise, Mydala.com. *Dala* in Sanskrit means group(s). I was headed to set up a group literally, in the Indian e-trading canvas."

Built on what essentially is a merchant marketing platform, Mydala helps businesses, especially service businesses, reach the right set of consumers. "When we started as a group buying deals site, we didn't realize the need that existed in the market for a marketing platform," observes the entrepreneur who set out to make history in the Indian web market. The deeper they explored the space, the greater depth of its potential was revealed. They founded their platform on the fact that in India, businesses such as small restaurants, salons, bakeries, or simply service providers of any sort, had very limited means to market themselves without spending a ridiculous amount of money first. "Now with over a hundred thousand retail businesses having used us as a platform in over 196 cities in India, we know that we are fulfilling a need," she admits with a sense of pride.

None of this came as easy as a click though. Back in 2009, when Mydala was taking baby steps, there were a lot of challenges that Anisha encountered. "People used to think I was handling two pregnancies at once," she jokes in recollection now. It was painstakingly difficult to run around for funds and handle her pregnancy at the same time. In the beginning, the now mother of two recalls, Mydala shared an office space with a dental clinic and they often held their meetings inside the clinic. "We had a hard time explaining to our potential candidates why the meetings were being held in that place. Now it just seems funny, but back then, I had a tough time convincing people to take us seriously and assuring them that we would grow into becoming a full-fledged, profit-churning organization." Anisha's venture into the waters of a fairly new trade space brought its own share of apprehensions and mistrust from otherwise extremely promising enterprises. However, with time and patience, things came around and they eventually stabilized with regular ecommerce.

It was the unending support of her family and friends that got this persevering tycoon through the initial storms. "I am lucky to have married my best friend and to have in-laws who support me through thick and thin," she reveals gratuitously. A firm believer in the power of karma, Anisha's mantra about facing her troubles was in her faith that all things happen in good time. And happen they did, as Mydala expanded with its reach and scale across the country, building recognition and strength that led to form a large family in itself. Mydala today stands with a strength of over four hundred employees consisting of teams which strive to achieve customer excellence. They have feet on the street and local presence in a hundred and fifty cities working with a sales manpower of over a hundred and fifty people. In her pursuit to ensuring excellence in service, Anisha ensures that attention and resources are dedicated primarily for customer satisfaction.

"Recently, we forayed into the grocery vertical with product listings from categories including eatables, personal care and household items. The users can search for all available products on the nearby supermarkets or *kirana* stores. It's doing very well and we will keep adding new features to this segment to keep the vertical sticky."

Her inherent understanding of technological application in ecommerce, and her experience in the aggressive international front of web marketing have brought her a long way as a leader of the segment. "We have a significant number of people working on developing the technology infrastructure which forms the backbone of our business. The analysis of user data from the merchant's perspective drives our revenue growth. With more and more merchants reaching customers using our platform, we are bound to gain priority in the consumer mindset. Needless to say, any consumer-facing business is backed by a strong customer service team," says the self-made businesswoman with a tone of ambitious determination.

Disappointment is not her cup of tea, Anisha has revealed that both in her performance with her organizations as well her attitude towards her customers. "We have a vigilant team dedicated to receiving feedback from our users through social media. But we have been lucky enough so far to not receive any major complaint regarding our services," she confesses humbly though one knows for sure that it has taken her a lot more than just good luck to build such a reputation for Mydala. Confident of her current position in the market as a business leader, she admits to not considering other rising enterprises in the realm as her competition. Although the likes of Justdial, Groupon and Coupondunia have built strong interfaces on the same lines, Anisha is determined to keep on her toes to stay ahead in the race.

Behind this voracious leader and entrepreneur is a mother and wife, affectionate and dedicated to her family. With an enigmatic balance between her professional and personal front, the trained Yoga instructor finds her true strength and confidence in the sunny smiles of her daughters. "My most gratifying moment was when my daughter told me that she was proud of me," she speaks candidly with an emotional spark in her eyes.

Whether it is work or home, the determined speculator invests liberally in her attention and intelligence, "My aim is to grow and evolve, always. If it is business, I want to keep exploring more exciting avenues to improve the enterprise. If it is family, I want to push my limits, making sure everyone grows and enjoys this process of living. This is something I do not compromise on," says the mother.

Ask her if she has future plans and she flashes a stunning, knowing smile that reveals she has it all mapped out.

"I want Mydala to be the de-facto service provider for loyalty programs and coupons, across the country. Everyone who enters the web market would come to us first!" she forecasts with a sense of pride and fortitude. The industry is filling fast with more innovative avenues that are invading the once monopolized arena of Mydala. Not only is the marketing aficionado well aware of its repercussions, but also embraces this as a challenge, an opportunity that she looks forward to. With a strong will to explore, experiment and evolve, she looks forward to both the challenges as well as the subsequent scope of evolution they offer.

The world is full of enterprising spirits – women who balance their work life and family. But dynamic women who celebrate and embrace such challenges are rare. Anisha has proved with her accomplishments of two successful businesses that such potential is both appreciable and achievable despite the most adverse circumstances. While living in no illusion of the stakes involved and hurdles expected, she personifies a will and commitment that inspires both women and men around the world. In pursuing what has been her dream and passion, she has earned the goodwill and blessings of all the small scale businesses across the country on the one hand, and a vast number of satisfied and continually progressing consumers on the other. Wrapping up her work, she walks out to meet her daughters who revolve as her strength and motivation. In her walking figure, Anisha reveals an aura of passion and perseverance, worth taking a note or two from.

Charnita Arora *came up with* **Perfect Life Spot** *to turn her dream of overall development of every student into reality. Currently, PLS stands proud as an institute of language and holistic development.*

The Perfect Spot for Life and Learning

Charnita Arora

Today's is a world that focuses on targets and numbers, trophies and victories, labels and appearances. From leaders of the top most organizations, to the students from most basic families, every one functions on these criteria. All our judgements, perceptions and deductions of success and failure, good and bad or right and wrong all evolve from this prevalent notion. While striving for excellence is the key to evolution, when excellence itself becomes a limitation that withholds motivation, we seriously need to reconsider our process of learning. Very few people in today's Indian system of education and learning understand this concept. A fewer still do anything about initiating a platform where learning can be redefined as a process of evolution rather than compartmentalized theories to be crammed for marks. However, in this trend of making education a business, there is a ray of hope in the form of a young thinker who has it in her motivated business to evolve a culture of learning that is experiential and elevating from within rather than selling out a patterned syllabus that is meant to feed minds with words and formulae.

Charnita Arora, a learner by spirit and teacher by profession, started with the concept of creating an environment that enunciates this very principle of learning. As an enthusiastic and unconventional scholar, she completed her bachelor's degree with Honours in English and went on to explore her journey in Germany, with the prestigious Erasmus Mundus Scholarship to pursue a Master's degree. This is where her journey towards self-discovery and insight both strengthened and deepened. With a quest for the secret to a peaceful, happy and healthy life, Charnita went on to study and experience the theories of many learned scholars like Thich Nhat Hanh, Richard Bach, Marshal Rosenberg, Sir Ken Robinson, Mihaly Csikszentmihalyi, and Joseph Campbell who inspired her to look at life and its learning from a deeper perspective. During this time, the enthusiastic writer had already started penning down her own ideas and learnings in the form of articles on her blog. It was her exposure to the best forms of education both external and internal that got her to reflect on the prevalent form of schooling in the Indian machinery.

"I started rigorously documenting ideas, anecdotes and concepts relating to the need for a more emotionally integrative system of education. I reimagined parenting as a psychologically-driven practice rather than only physiologically-driven," she explains with reflection on how thoughts transpired into words. Charnita's experience as an assistant professor in the Delhi University was a close encounter with the conventional pattern of delivery of knowledge. "I got a chance to reflect on the kind of opportunity and necessity there is for an evolutionary method of learning, considering the limitations of our present system of education," she explains.

That she had to be involved intimately with education and the cycle of teaching and learning was certain. But her dissatisfaction with the schooled, degreed and marks-oriented label of learning lead her to form her own parallel. Even while teaching in DU, the experimentalist would often bring along her laptop and projector to break the conventional top down approach of imparting education and would attempt to make it more interactive and experiential. A process that was motivated towards experiential learning, towards emotional strengthening along with the academic and was based strongly on the principle of non-violent communication in education eventually lead into the establishment of Perfect Life Spot (PLS), Charnita's offering to the society as a place where the very style of learning is dedicated to a holistic development of the individual.

"I really believe that for true learning to happen, the learner must feel emotionally safe and positive. Hence, I followed Marshall Rosenberg's ideas on non-judgmental/non-violent communication," she explains the founding principle of Perfect Life Spot. Creating an environment which is warm, respectful to emotions, and encourages learning through experiencing. PLS works as a platform for teaching English language and important employability/life skills to young adults aged between seventeen to twenty-four years. More than merely being an academic substitute, PLS is a journey of self-discovery and self-actualization of each and every individual. "We work with small batches of about ten-fifteen members in each group, so that everyone gets focused attention and a chance to be heard, something that lacks tremendously in our prevalent education system," she comments.

Talking about a serious crisis of self-confidence and self-love in the students of today, Charnita stresses on the need for nurturing lives through education in the form of healing experiences rather than severing them through fierceness of competitions and labels.

"It has to be non-judgmental and non-violent. That's exactly what is missing fundamentally in today's society and we can't afford to propagate that in our very education," she voices her concern. Quoting the many instances of students not feeling comfortable expressing their feelings, or lacking confidence in accepting their personalities, she goes on to explain the damage caused because of superlatives of comparisons attached to our judgement towards students and how PLS tries to repair such damages in an encouraging and expressive environment. Games, activities and learning through experiences are ways in which she conducts her workshops with the youth and helps them reinstate the enthusiasm and eagerness to learn for the sake of evolving. Today, every single child that takes part in the sessions in Perfect Life Spot has found new and more meaningful definitions of education. Not only are they emotionally stronger, but have statistically shown major improvements in their academic performances as well! This only goes on to strengthen Charnita's belief in her ideology of transforming the formal education system in India.

Speaking of challenges, Perfect Life Spot has had its share of hurdles in the path of reaching its current state of recognition and acceptance, both at the ideological as well as entrepreneurial level. "It was difficult for people in general to understand the need for something like PLS," she recalls. "It wasn't a school, it wasn't a conventional coaching institute either, so parents couldn't initially relate with the concept of this form of education."

While struggling with clearing ideological misconceptions about PLS, Charnita was also fighting another stereotypical challenge posed before her through the Indian mindset. Being a woman who was trying to set her feet in the entrepreneurial work frame did not receive a welcoming response. "As if being a woman was not enough, my politeness was also assumed as a sign of weakness. This goes on to explain a lot about how aggressive and dominant we are as a society and how misconstrued our notions of power are," she reflects insightfully. But it was the outer challenges that helped the spiritual explorer find her inner peace and motivation. Having discovered the basics of what was going wrong with the society, she was inspired to change it at the fundamental level of education through non aggressive and non-violent methods of interaction.

Along with sessions and workshops for students, PLS conducts offline as well as online courses in Mindfulness and Emotional well-being for Corporate audiences. A firm believer in constant growth and evolution, Charnita also diversifies and enlarges her impact circle with the intention of touching many more lives and helping out people in crisis.

"This year I noticed the rising rate in youth suicide, which is why we decided to include teenagers as young as thirteen years of age into our sessions. I know mental and emotional healing can make a big difference in such cases so we shouldn't hold back," she speaks compassionately. "The most difficult person to impress is you, and once you have managed to accomplish that, nothing can put you down!" Corresponding to the growth of her reach, Charnita has also expanded the resource hub from being a singular writer in blogs to a family of several awakened members who form her reliable team. Having trained over a hundred facilitators equipped in the dimension of mindfulness and non-aggressive, experiential learning, Perfect Life Spot has collaborated with several schools and corporates now and continues to propagate the evolutionary form of education.

"At the core, we have a six member team and we all work together in the verticals of ecosystem-management content and research, marketing and partnership-building, counseling and guidance, facilitation and mentoring skills. And it is our sincere aim to grow, learn and evolve both at the individual, as well as the organizational level."

Reflecting on the journey, Charnita talks about the experience of being a persistent learner which makes her an efficient teacher. A strong believer in experiencing every moment of the path rather than the mere destination, she shares her passion that makes Perfect Life Spot so special for her.

"It's not just a business opportunity for me. I could have worked at stable organizations for that if it was about making a career. It is my journey of self-actualization and reflection that inspires me to find that place in life that blossoms happiness in my thoughts and actions. And once I have found that, I have realized that many people can also understand and benefit from the same. This experiencing and sharing is what Perfect Life Spot means to me," she smiles with a glint of inner peace in her eyes. It makes a big difference to live your passion grow into an experience you can share with others; it has meant a lot to Charnita too. "It moves me to see the reaction of these students at the end of the sessions. It's like an instant connection of the soul that shakes you up from inside. This makes me feel that the road I have chosen is taking me on a meaningful journey."

The transformation in the participants is visible both at the level of their emotional evolution, as well as the level of their performance in their respective spheres. Anshul, who took a course with Perfect Life Spot last year explains her experience here as enchanting. "This institution has helped me rub off the dust imposed by myself over the years of harsh realities and the world of grown ups through very simple and funflilled learning!" she reveals. From weekend workshops on self-acceptance, mind-management, emotional intelligence, healing your childhood, coping with stress, to weekday batches which cater to undergraduate English Literature guidance, these courses seek to inculcate assertiveness, self-acceptance and confidence in each individual according to their needs.

"Once you enter the institute, you can feel it...the energy... the peace of mind. And once you are done with the class, you hear a voice inside you telling you that you can achieve anything," says Sakshi who gives PLS a five-star rating.

For the year 2016, Queens Young Leaders program selected Charnita for a program called 'Leading Change' conducted by the University of Cambridge. She was also the winner of Science Slam 2014, where her paper on the need for Digital Mindfulness (the way we use internet and how it affects our lives) got selected for a prestigious scholarship from German House of Research and Innovation. Not just that, she is a voracious writer on topics of well-being for well-known publications like *Elite Daily, Elephant Journal, Business World,* among others. Her recent TEDx talk on the vital issues she addresses with her students everyday has become another feather in her cap.

Setting a foundation that is bringing about small but significant revolutions in the lives of people, Charnita is an embodiment of inspiration that breaks conventions of the notions of business, career or even definitions of success. As a philanthropic thinker and perpetual learner, she has set new parameters of education. Institutions and organizations across the country can learn a lot from this model, not only in terms of the methods of delivery, but in redefining what motivates education and formal learning processes in the country. It is her aim to create an environment for each one to discover their worth and motivation and to simply find their own perfect spots of life and learning.

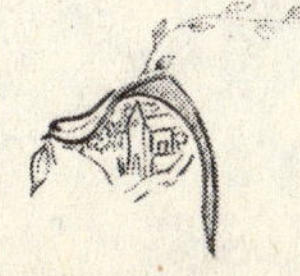

More than merely being an academic substitute, this Delhi-based institution is in itself a journey of self-realization for each individual.

Falak Randerian *is an avid reader herself and her brainchild* **My Little Chatterbox** *helps encourage children develop healthy reading habits. The lending library called The Reading Room offers a selection of handpicked books.*

All in her Good Books

Falak Randerian

In the world of over-worked professions, there are people who carve their own niche through ideas that affect this fast-spreading madness in ways that help add value. For children, specially, when an opportunity like this sprouts, it's not in plenty, and especially not one that most parents can afford to miss. Falak Randerian is one such person who is a glimmer of hope that is spreading silently with a cause and effect, echoing a story that speaks a thousand truths about its impact.

That she would one day build an enterprise of her own, was known to her long before she took the first step. It truly combined two of her passions – her addiction to books and reading, and her affection for children. The amalgamation of her desire to begin her own business and her passion gave birth to what has now become a beautiful world called My Little Chatterbox. As a start-up, it engaged children in communication workshops, but soon dived into creating a platform for book clubs and lessons in phonetics.

"My Little Chatterbox believes in the power of reading and books. Children need activities that are fun and creative, which fuel their imagination, keep them busy and leave potential for more…books do just that and more," explains Falak with absolute cognizance of a child's needs. With a vision to create a relationship between children and books that lasts a lifetime, the reading enthusiast launched My Little Chatterbox in 2012. This all happened ten years into her professional life when Falak became a mom and took a break from her job. "The experience brought me closer to children, and gave me time to reflect on things I like to do. Books, naturally, were the first choice," she reveals about the genesis of the unique reading club.

A firm believer in hard work, Falak had started building My Little Chatterbox when she was thirty. With a strong educational and vocational background, she holds a degree in Corporate Communication and is a certified Phonetics trainer from Jolly Learning, UK. Having years of experience as a communication expert across platforms, the bold risk taker began what is now trending as a popular book club culture in Bangalore. The enterprise had once started with sessions in libraries and activity centres but has now become a popular hub for young ones with a functional centre of its own launched last year. Along with the objective of encouraging youngsters to read and associate with books, My Little Chatterbox also offers a unique platform for children to collectively understand phonics and grammar, creating a holistic experience of reading and sharing knowledge from books. Taking the opportunity one step further, the service is also now penetrating through the franchise model, hence reaching out to a wider audience in the city. With three years of functionality, My Little Chatterbox is now a popular choice with good recommendations from parents and schools alike and comes as a welcome relief of productive engagement in times where children are engaged in video games and technological entertainment.

A concept so unique in its foundation has clearly not been set on easy grounds. Challenges had been plenty on ground zero,

"It was difficult to explain the concept to my parents at that time, when even the concept of coming together to read books was not a popular one," Falak speaks in reminiscence, "but I was willing to go the extra mile and keep a patient head because I was confident that once the idea hit home, it would be a success!"

Even at the stage of planning and initiation, she was ready with her homework and a mindset to face failures and challenges as they came.

"Raising funds was a major challenge, especially as a woman in this country," she continues. "Women in my family are not known to work after becoming mothers. It was a difficult idea for them to accept when they got to know I was setting my own business."

Money and business came slow in the initial phase for the lone captain of the enterprise. As funding was and still continues to be a major challenge, she initially used her own savings to invest in the business. In every sense, this has been her child.

Notwithstanding the odds against the business, Falak struggled on as a one woman army. But thankfully, she was not alone in life to face the struggle. "My father passed away while I was still in college, in 2003. He was and still continues to be my greatest source of support and inspiration," she reveals with serene acceptance. Finding her strength in her husband, she goes on with gratitude about his unconditional love and backing, something that has helped her grow as an entrepreneur, a wife and a mother.

"I work till late in the night so my daughter spends time with her father in the morning. But she spends time with me while I am at the centre till she is put to bed. My time is sincerely dedicated between work and family, both of which are my strengths," she explains the perfect balance she maintains as an ambitious business woman and a responsible wife and mother.

Marching ahead with My Little Chatterbox, the avid reader attributes its success to its one-of-a-kind creativity and dedication that has earned goodwill over the years. "It's primarily word of mouth that speaks for our credibility," she reflects on her strategic growth with every milestone. Starting with sporadic sessions on communication, it has been service of high quality and Falak's commitment that has earned My Little Chatterbox a reputation that most parents want to associate with. With steady revenue coming in from training sessions and franchises, the enterprise is now all set to venture into its star element, The Reading Room, which is a library cum reading lounge where children can come, read or even borrow books through a membership. This is a platform for parents to come together and learn ways to raise readers, as is the fundamental aim of My Little Chatterbox.

A walk down the memory lane brings back to her mind the first session of My Little Chatterbox.

"There were mistakes I made; I was also a little nervous. It was the first step of my business after all!" she reflects candidly. Thinking of the mistakes and feedback as a stepping stone to evolution, she admits to having no regrets in this fascinating journey so far. Positive and content with the way her life has been going, Falak is determined to take the platform to a wider, bigger audience across the country. "I am happy with the response I get from people. They reach us through people who have availed our service, or through social media. So the interaction is mostly very personal." With a vision to expand at a national level, Falak feels confident and certain that things will only head forward from here. "It is always the clients that have approached us so far. We haven't had the need to run after people to get more business. It is inspiring to observe that what we deliver is not only accepted but also promoted by our clients," she declares with a sense of achievement.

Milestones have been plenty in the small span of the constantly growing platform. From sessions in activity centres to building their own centre, diversifying into MLCB Phonics and preparing for The Reading Room, the achievements have been numerous.

"It feels really great to see My Little Chatterbox grow like this," she exclaims with pride, "and when I see little children develop skills in sessions, or when parents come over to express their satisfaction, I know my hard work is paying off."

With ambitions to expand and root deeper into the ground, Falak is all set with her launch of the library. "So far it's been only me handling all aspects of the business, but I think My Little Chatterbox is ready to take the next few steps now."

With a plan to hire at least five more people in the team by this year, the dynamic business woman is already planning ahead with goals and the direction she needs to steer towards.

"When I had first started My Little Chatterbox, it was a brand new idea, a concept nobody had heard of before. But as people started accepting and appreciating the concept, many others also have tried to ape the model for their own business." With a small hint of disappointment veiling through her voice, Falak honestly expresses her angst at the situation. With book clubs mushrooming every now and then in the city, she has gracefully accepted that competition has considerably increased but however agrees that credit must be acknowledged for the hard work and creativity where it's due, a phenomenon she finds scarce in her sector. "It doesn't matter how tough the competition gets, my endeavour is to always stay one step ahead, to always feed creativity and enthusiasm, just like the motto of My Little Chatterbox." Her confidence and sincerity reflect in not only the fast-rising popularity of MLCB but also in the words of those who have experienced benefits in their children.

"My son joined MLCB Phonics before he turned four and by the time he finished at four-and-a-half years, he could read and figure out spellings like a pro. The classes were fun and he would look forward to attend these classes. Falak doesn't force kids but she has a way with them," praises an enthusiastic parent whose child participated in the sessions this year. With responses like these, Falak is motivated to ask for more interaction with parents and children to get a better understanding of what's working and what isn't.

"Taking feedback in the right spirit is extremely essential. As long as it's genuine, I take criticism as a serious source of learning, something I have evolved to adopt over the years," acclaims Falak.

What started with the love for books and children has now grown into a platform that entices and excites many lives in the progressive city of Bangalore. When Falak was featured in the *Women's Web* article 'Thirty Incredible Indian Women Entrepreneurs', it was no surprise. Not only has she been on a consistent rise in the world of business development, but has been affecting lives across diversity of ages. Every single session, with every child has not only been an experience with books and reading, but has contributed into cultivating a lifestyle that encourages learning, exploring and evolving into what will hopefully last for a lifetime. Not only are the children benefitting from this sort of lucrative exposure, but the parents themselves have found a great deal of benefit in their lives, and in their relationships with their children. Falak encourages women across the country to be enterprising and to take the leap of faith, only asking of them to be sincere, hardworking and ready to take failures in the same stride as success. She stands tall as an inspiring entrepreneur, a creative thinker, a loving mother and an empowered woman – a life which has pages full of examples for people to read and follow.

Geetika Chadha *is a certified image management graduate and puts her knowledge and experience as an image consultant to assist and empower individuals and organizations to be their own masterpiece through* **Imagenie**.

Masterpiece at Work

Geetika Chadha

"You can either be a part of the problem, or the solution," she says with an air of serene positivity about her tone. Looking at the young and high-spirited girl at the first go, you can't really make out the depth of insight and experience she has at such a young age. But under the layers of youth lies motivation and perseverance that has inspired and motivated many to discover their mettle. She understands what it takes for people to find themselves; she recognizes that which most people are looking for. For people to find motivation, it is important for them to feel the force from within. For some, it comes in the form of their work, for others, in finding their true calling and for some special ones, just finding who they are is enough to inspire them into becoming powerful. It's like lighting up a candle, and passing on the flame and its aura to everyone around. As much as it is for igniting one's own direction, it is equally responsible for showing others the path to strength and success. Building on this need of the people around her, blended with her drive and skill to recreate people's images of themselves, Geetika has set out on a certain way of life. Reflecting exactly what she is in her work, the bright entrepreneur is a proud owner of one of India's most popular and most revolutionary business models and has carved her own niche. This enterprise has risen from being an experiment with a non-existent future to becoming a space of popular choice of some of the most prominent people in the country.

A growing up Geetika was like any other ordinary girl. With her family roots in Haryana, she moved to the capital of the country to pursue her bachelors in Computer Science from Miranda House – one of most reputed colleges of Delhi University. Geetika's father is a traditional agriculturist and her mother, an affectionate and dedicated home-maker. Having lived in a typical Indian household as a growing adult, she is the youngest of the four daughters of the family and has a younger brother. Experimental and experiential by nature, the young learner has always aimed to try new things and find happiness in the simple joys of life. Always the studious academician, Geetika was expected to choose and ace the popular vocational choices by both the society and her family. The fate, and her own fire, however, had different plans for the eager explorer. After completing her graduation, Geetika was offered one of the best placement jobs of her batch in the magnanimous city of Hyderabad. At the same time, she also received her acceptance letter from National Institute of Fashion Technology, Hyderabad. It was a tough call for the young girl torn between the security of a well paying job and opening doors of her dream. Always a huge fan of aesthetics and creativity, Geetika's heart was in styling, but her parents and conventions expected of her to take the safer road. However, having made up her mind about the road she wanted to take, Geetika headed out to the campus in the city of Nizams to embrace her fate. "I still remember when my father and I had reached the college campus. The office I had been placed at was at the opposite side of the college gates. He asked me even then if I wanted to turn around and not take the job. He wanted to make sure that my confidence and assertion in my choices was strong," she recollects the dilemma of her early stages. However, once the decision was made, destiny came out with open arms to support her and blossom her skills into professional perfection. And in all the decisions she took thereafter, Geetika found unconditional support and approval from her parents.

The first few jobs came from the top fashion and retail brands of the country and it is here that Geetika ripened in her experience of organizations and the world of business, inadvertently preparing herself for the opportunity awaiting her in the future.

Destined to come back to where it had all began, Geetika found herself back in Hyderabad after marrying her soulmate Avish, a businessman whom she had met by chance in Delhi. "After coming to Hyderabad, there weren't many options in organized retail and the fashion industry. I was contemplating on the kind of work I wanted to do and Image Consulting was the answer," she shares about the initial crisis. A brain child of detailed deliberation of the enterprising couple, the concept of starting an image consultancy came as a result of Geetika's deep desire to work on styling and a huge scope in the market with this unconventional genre. All these factors, clubbed with Geetika's perseverance and intelligence, led into forming what is today known as India's leading image consultancy and makeover service, Imagenie.

"Our aim is to help people discover the best versions of them. We equip them with the 'life skill' of creating their 'personal brand' by managing their appearance, etiquette, body language and communication," she explains the ethos of Imagenie. With the concept of empowering people into believing in themselves, and portraying a convincing and powerful image to the outside world, the ingenious enterprise works through a series of individual consultations and group workshops or trainings. "Imagenie is for everybody, from a five-year-old kid to a fifty-year-old person – everybody who needs help in finding themselves," she speaks with a warm smile. With a tagline that encourages personal creativity and control, Imagenie inspires styling and confidence in the words – 'Be your own masterpiece'.

Walking into unknown waters was indeed a challenge for the enterprising leader in the beginning. But as someone who nicknames hurdles as 'fun', Geetika made the best of the challenges and found innovative methods to enhance her business as an image consultant. "It's fun when some last minute fixes while styling become fashion statements, while at times the last minute glitches create problems. But in the end, it's all fun!" she exclaims. Describing the journey, she talks about how Imagenie had started receiving work and enquiries even before the brand had been properly established.

"Working with my first client was the most memorable experience. It was a makeover that taught me a lot, and helped me set the foundation stones for the rest of the journey," she reflects. Working for a newly-promoted vice president of a reputed organization, Geetika helped the lady create a powerful professional impression. The inner and outer transformation brought about through Imagenie brought about a major change in her perception of life. "It is so gratifying that such efforts can bring about very evident changes in people, their attitude and in their life altogether. It's not like I am finishing one project after another, it's more like I am getting involved in the fabric of people's lives and helping them weave it in the way they want." Looking back at time when everything from funding to promoting was uncertain, it was the dynamic revolution in Geetika's spirit that spoke with confidence. She was certain that if she offered her idea and service in the right manner, there would be no dearth of takers. And she did prove herself right in reaching a stage in her business today where top personalities from different disciplines reach out to her for their inner and outer transformation.

"There are so many layers to a person – from their innermost feelings to their outer appearances. I have worked with some of the top celebrities and it's a great experience to polish each of their layers. It's a new lesson for me each time," she reveals with true appreciation of her passion.

Ask Geetika if she had ever imagined coming this far with her own story and she smiles with knowing confidence. The travelling enthusiast always knew she had journeys to make on her own, "I always knew I wanted an office of my own. However tedious and unpredictable it has been, I have completely enjoyed putting my hundred percent into it." Although entrepreneurship comes naturally to her, Geetika calls it a 24x7 job. Being her own boss never allows her to take time off. But having a husband who understands and runs his business prosperously has been a boon for her in the long run. Even in her personal world, Geetika lives with complete dedication and creativity. "We share the same interests and passion, both at work and in our personal lives," she reveals about her life with Avish.

"Maintaining work and home balance is the mantra of our marriage, which is why we stand up for each other, no matter what."

Extending her warmth and relations beyond boundaries of professional parameters, Geetika explains the success of Imagenie as a result of the strong support from her husband. From helping me make decisions, to supporting me on issues ranging from emotions to expenditure, Avish helped me grow my entrepreneurial child into its current stature," she speaks with affection about her husband and the support he gave her.

Reforming the way you look, whether it's your appearance or perspective, has been the key essence of Imagenie and its founder. As someone who finds joy in the simpler things of life, Geetika quotes her proud moments in this journey as time spent with every person, helping them achieve a desired versions of themselves. "When you see how you have touched the lives of people, and the things they will remember you for, you feel like you're on the right track. It's a win-win situation for everybody, isn't it?"

In her philanthropic approach to people and life in general, Geetika looks at people respectfully. When she had started with the idea of image consultancy, it was an unheard concept, but today many people have started working in this field with different objectives and methodologies. Not the sort to feel insecure easily, Geetika considers competition as healthy motivation and appreciates them for all the different and unique methods they have introduced in the world of image consultancy.

"Now I don't need to sit content with our current position, but to innovate and evolve because of the competition. Isn't that just the perfect excuse to learn and grow?"

With growth as her motivation mantra, Geetika plans expansion and innovation in image consultancy and plans to work further in movie styling. "I have a platform that has reached out to many people. They are not only a mark of my success but a very effective means of advertising for me. Through them, the ethos of Imagenie spreads to other people and helps me to reach and help out many more lives," she reveals with a mature understanding of business. What started as a desire to pursue her love for aesthetics and culture took shape of a revolution in the Indian space of enterprises. Today, not only has Geetika helped many discover new and better versions of them but also inspired and supported many people to live with confidence and face the world with newfound enthusiasm. While her confidence and perseverance has been exemplary, Geetika, through her own journey, has also motivated young and creative aspirants to stand up with their ideas, no matter how unique and offbeat they may sound, and pursue them with confidence. In the true sense, she is building masterpieces and inspiring people to work on their own masterpieces as well!

Pankhuri Shrivastava *started* **GrabHouse** *as an online platform where both landlords and tenants could post their requirements, without any brokerage or fee.*

Home is where Grabhouse is!

Pankhuri Shrivastava

It is rare that parents of little children encourage them to find their own wings, and when they do, it results in inspiring a spirit in the young ones that would change their perspective towards life altogether. In a social set-up that is dedicated to following the predictable path, whether it is in professional or personal choices, there are very few people who follow their hearts and dare to move out of conventional paths. When such efforts bear fruit with heartfelt dedication and passion for one's work, the results are not only outstanding in themselves, but also create ripples that influence people around with the benefits. One such girl who was encouraged by her parents as a child also formed her perceptions to look beyond conventions and conditions, and in turn created ripples that have affected thousands of individuals and families.

A graduate with B.E. in Computer Science from the bustling city of Bhopal, Pankhuri had the world of possibilities before her as a growing up teenager. From sports to theatre, dancing to singing, academics to volunteering, she explored all verticals of interest with the generous support of her parents.

"I was always exposed to a plethora of activities, always encouraged to take chances and not hesitate from trying out new things. That has always motivated me to take risks and has brought me a long way," expresses the versatile learner. Even after her graduation, she was offered with the option of either pursuing her MBA from a top B school of the country, or volunteering as a teacher for one of India's largest and most impactful children's education programmes. The easier choice for her would have been to take up her Master's degree and attain a lucrative and stable job like the rest of her peers. However, the daring experimenter chose to volunteer with the non-government organization for two years instead! Unpredictable, unprecedented and seemingly illogical – the move seemed just that to many around Pankhuri, but she had her mind made up.

"I can do an MBA whenever I want, but I know for sure that getting to work at the grass-root level with children in this conventional manner was not something I would have stumbled upon every day, so I took my leap of faith," she recollects the drastic decision that changed everything. Two years as a teacher taught Pankhuri a lot more than she had expected. Learning to be flexible and adaptive, and to stay in the problem-solving mode instead of complaining about problems, are some of the priceless attributes she mastered in her experience in the two wonderful years teaching children. As a consequence, when she came out of the fellowship, Pankhuri was ready to start something of her own, perhaps without experience of business or complete knowledge of the tact of enterprises, but with absolute confidence, faith and the will to explore possibilities.

Her explorative spirit got her to diving into the housing situation of the country, specially the metropolitan cities. "When an individual or a family wanted to move into a new city, or even a new locality in the same city, they did not have any organized facility to connect them to possible choices. The most common option was to go through brokers who'd charge a significant amount for their service," she explains the market gap that inspired her venture. As a solution, Pankhuri decided to start her own digital portal that could be used by both landlords as well as tenants to post their requirements respectively. This completely eliminated the involvement of any broker and practically connected the two sources without extra cost or hassles! Thus started a revolution in the real estate transaction in a creative, digitized and accessible model called Grabhouse, started by Pankhuri when she was merely twenty-three.

Just as whacky and unconventional the idea of Grabhouse, so is its name. As someone who loves the idea of names, Pankhuri was excited about starting her own brand. Pankhuri is an embodiment of her own name, reflecting her free spirit and exploratory flight. In the same way, Grabhouse, she explains is a platform where you can find a house very quickly. "It sounds fun, creative and specific to the services it offers, which is why after going through thousands of names, this stuck and stayed on," she speaks enthusiastically. Currently functional in seven metro cities – Mumbai, Bangalore, Pune, Delhi NCR, Kolkata, Chennai and Hyderabad – the online enterprise has supported thousands of seekers in finding houses within their specific requirements of design, budget and locality, all that without the extra brokerage charges.

In principle, it may seem simplistic and easy to formulate into action. But in reality, Grabhouse has seen its share of struggles in the foundation years. "Getting funding in the initial phase was a challenge as our profit generation wouldn't come immediately. This was a risk I had understood before starting out," she explains. Along with her co-founder Prateek Shukla, the young entrepreneur managed to raise funds amounting to thirteen million dollars in three rounds, through some of the most prominent brands around. "It's exciting to see such reputed investors showing faith in our revolutionary model. This not only goes on to speak volumes about the potential of the business, but also works as a major confidence booster for us as a young start-up team," she confesses happily.

Networking has been a challenge for Pankhuri as a woman entrepreneur in a country that is neither comfortable nor welcoming to women in business. "Often my rapport building is mistaken by many potential clients and funders as something more personal. This attitude is disappointing and disturbing as well." She goes on to share her challenges candidly, "I am sure if I were a man, the conversations would have been taken as strictly professional." However, embracing risks with a positive attitude and a well-prepared mindset, Pankhuri does not let shocks affect her. "There's a lot at stake, because people have faith in me, have invested money, time and energy, and so all those expectations have to be met each day. But I take that with a bright spirit, as a challenge I have to embrace every day," she shares insightfully. The daring dynamite has worked around the hurdles of a start-up to attain acceptance and popularity not only with the online presence of Grabhouse, but also with the parallel business model that connects her with other enterprises and funders. After having become a popular portal for house seekers, Pankhuri launched a profit generating design in the venture. "We offer a choice to Grabhouse users to opt for privileged services, which is a paid service for getting multiple options, assisted service and help with moving in. This is the core revenue model which is complemented with other profit-generating channels." The once young start-up has also grown in its structure and strength. From a team of two risking partners to a significant family of eighty members, Grabhouse has talents working from across the country. "Mostly comprising of developers, designers and product evangelists, the Grabhouse team has its own communication and operations strategy team as well," she speaks with a sense of satisfied accomplishment. Having started as someone who had no experience or degree in business management, Pankhuri has come a long way. And yet, humble in gratitude, she attributes this recognition and success to everyone on the team, from her partner to the newest employees, who have all contributed in their dimensions into adding talent and value to the organization.

A woman who gives importance on the journey rather than the destination, Pankhuri feels thankful for all the lessons, whether academic or experiential, that have brought her this far. From being brought up by a pair of radical parents, to availing every opportunity, to her in-depth education in computer science – all lessons have been important assets in making her what she is today. "My understanding of technology has been the backbone of the online portal. This helps me immensely in figuring out what is going right in the website and what are the innovations I can incorporate to keep the services evolving." She talks about the move that changed the traditional house hunting norm with creative technology. Breaking away from the conventions seems to be the mantra in both Pankhuri's work as well as her philosophy. With respect to enterprising women in a predominantly male hemisphere, she believes the time to change this culture has come. Focusing on professional excellence as well as personal accomplishments is what she encourages, especially understanding the circumstances of a woman employee. "I am happy to say that 40% of our employees are women; this is a significant number considering a technical team is conventionally composed of men. However, in the coming months, I aim to take this number even higher," she adds aspiringly. Having promoted a philosophy of opportunity and creativity amidst her team members, Pankhuri proudly speaks about how not a single person from the starting of Grabhouse has left the organization till date, the fact in itself speaking lengths about the ethos of the venture in both its quality and principles.

The trained Kathak dancer and singer, Pankhuri is a dynamic human being with versatile interests. In her personal life, just as her professional domain, she believes in freedom of exploration and innovation. When at home, she is surrounded by her own library of books which she holds accountable for having taught her most of the important lessons of life. In her free time, she is either nurturing some of her hobbies, or exploring the latest digital developments. 'The born leader' as her family calls her, enjoys spending time with her parents who still continue to encourage her to explore new paths. Despite being intensely attached to them, she believes in exercising her own responsibilities and rights, whether they are work related financial requirements or personal decisions.

Speaking of life-changing decisions, the avid reader speaks fondly of Grabhouse as her dream come true. Having surpassed the bigger challenges, whether financial, managerial or even personal, Pankhuri today stands tall with her strength, inspiring her team towards excellence. "There are a lot of things that I have learnt from this journey, especially from my mistakes," she explains. "Basic things like outsourcing to a third party can make you lose control of things, you need to be ready and cautious of that." Having mended and built the enterprise bit by bit, she feels proud of the success that has come with the hard work. Watching the entire team work together as committed individuals brings her absolute satisfaction. A firm believer in the power of goodwill and positive energy, she strives to radiate the same amidst her co-workers each morning after setting daily goals and appreciating achievements, big or small! With her eyes set on the future, Pankhuri aims for Grabhouse to expand to all the major cities of the country and redefine traditional house searching hassle into an experience of fun and comfort. "Things are changing fast in today's world with technology. We have tapped the right portal in this change and come this far, but there's a lot more to be done, higher mountains to be scaled," she declares ambitiously. Not like the heights of the mountains she has scaled already is anything less than noteworthy. Pankhuri humbly shares her proudest moments as benchmarks of achievements for Grabhouse. Whether it was reaching the 10,000 user mark in less than a year, or having helped customers save crores of rupees on brokerage, or witnessing the magic of a 100% team loyalty when they shifted base from Mumbai to Bangalore, the emotional and financial achievements have humbled her to strive for excellence. "When we raised funds from the best venture capitalists across the globe and proved that a user focused model can make a place of its own in a crowded market, it was a great morale booster for the entire team. There's so much gratitude for the success that has brought us so far," she speaks with humility.

Still deeply connected with her voluntary education program, Pankhuri's heart reaches out empathetically for all the children she can reach out to. If not Grabhouse, she would have still found herself spending time with the children of municipal schools in Mumbai, where the heart-changing process for her began. "There's so much to do in this world, so many people to reach. We all need to step up and take the leap of faith," she speaks soulfully. Assessing the situation of the women entrepreneurs in the country, she hopes to be able to inspire them in any way possible.

"You have to realize that right now is the best time! Whether you are single, or married, or a mother, there's nothing that can stop you if you make up your mind to do something good." Her inspiring words resonate through her actions in many lives. For the lives she has touched in helping them find homes, and for the lives she has inspired to break through from comforts of conventions, Pankhuri stands as an example of a sincere flight of faith and passion.

Heads Up For Tails *is a loved brainchild of* **Rashi Narang** *that arose out of the need to provide essential as well as exclusive merchandise for pets.*

Petting One's Dreams

Rashi Narang

Our areas of interest often go on to define the roads we take, the work we do or the people we become. More often than not, our actions give us the satisfaction of personal achievement, and in a sense, inspire us to carry things forward in our own spaces. However, there are a few beings of passion who expand their areas of interests into what becomes a phenomenon, a rage of sorts. This is the story of one such passionate entrepreneur who found her calling in her furry bundle of joy, and went on to create a significant evolution in the way pet parents and their pets can find fun, convenience and comfort in their everyday lives.

Rashi Narang, who started out on her own road to create her own business at an early age of twenty-five years is a name that has appeared time and again for her conspicuous efforts to initiate and improve the lifestyle of pets in Indian families. The erstwhile Human Resource team member in a reputed organization in London explains her transformation of career choices as a result of her profound realization.

"I had a dream job, something I had worked hard for right after my college and I had no reason to complain. But after a few months of working there, I realized that this was not where my heart was," she speaks in retrospection. This realization was her first step to actualizing her vision of starting something of her own. "Something big, original and unique. I wanted to do something that would make a difference."

Rashi's quest for her cause brought her across an array of opportunities in London as well as in India, when she moved back after her wedding. She worked with schools for underprivileged children for a while in her pursuit to do something meaningful and productive for her ecology.

But it was only her intimate experience with her own pet, Sara, that she realized her true and undying passion and love for animals, "Pets had always been a member of my family, one way or another, but it was Sara who came into my life to give me the experience of assuming responsibility of our furry friends," she explains with parent-like affection in her voice. In taking care of her beloved friend, the young seeker realized that the Indian market did not serve to the needs of pets and their parents/caregivers in the way a family member needed. The more she went out to explore utility and recreational options for Sara, the more she was exposed to this huge gap in the market for pet care products. It was then that Rashi determined to take things into her hands and attempted to bridge this gap. This determination, born out of concern and love, led to the foundation of what has now become one of the most recognized brands for pet care in India, fondly named as Heads Up For Tails.

A platform that celebrates pets and all the joy that they bring in our lives, Heads Up for Tails offers a vast range of fun, functional and useful merchandise for pets to help enhance their lifestyles.

Its ingenuity lies in the creative and effective range of products it offers that are available to customization to suit the needs and fancies of pet parents and their intuitive friends of fur. Products ranging from orthopedic beds to personalized collars, health products to fashionable accessories and apparel, all created with personal attention and unique designs make up the collection of the retail range.

"I am a pet parent and I understand the needs of Sara, I understand the heartfelt concerns I have for her, and things I like to do for her as her caregiver. It was this emotion that I poured into my trade, which my target audience needs and can relate with. This has been the backbone of Heads Up For Tails."

She talks about the ethos of her enterprise with pride. The fun and unique name for the products goes on to reflect on the spirit it vouches for – a cause that supports animal care and is unique, fun and creative in its services.

Starting with only a single product back in the year 2008, Heads Up For Tails began as an enterprise run from home by a one woman army. Venturing initially only as an online store, the reach and response of products encouraged Rashi to open her retail stores within a year of the brand's genesis – an achievement that speaks tons for a start-up company initiated single handedly. Soon, customer feedback and demands for more products started pouring in generously, leading into service diversification. Within a couple of years, Rashi's baby business had blossomed into a range of products including personalized collars, apparels, accessories, the pet bandanas and healthcare products like fruit based biscuits that are healthy and wholesome, and have yet not found a parallel in the market in terms of their quality. Taking things further, Rashi also found a way to fill a gap for creating health conscious and environment friendly jute toys that promise to harm neither the animals, nor the environment during or after usage. Her concern for the entire ecosystem has made itself evident in her attention to minute details, and her awareness towards the need of the environment.

"We create and sell products that simply help to treat pets better. We believe that they are just as much a part of the family, and deserve the attention and luxury that we provide for other family members."

Speaking of her premium clothing range for pets, she talks about the fairness of fashion that they should not be deprived of. Offering designer jackets, sherwanis and trendy apparel for pets, Rashi caters to fashion conscious families who know better than to dress their quadruped friends in table cloths! Laying stress on quality and utility, she ensures that the range of products offered, including the martingale collars and soft training tools keep in mind the safety and comfort of its users.

What may seem like a flourishing tale of happy tails now has seen its moments of crisis in the last seven years of stumbling, seeking, learning and stabilizing. It wasn't an easy start for Rashi, considering how niche and how new the market was. It was difficult to convince people initially that this could work.

"My parents were concerned about the relevance of such an idea in the Indian market, though they continued to hold faith in me nonetheless."

The early years were not easy in terms of market understanding or funding either. "I invested whatever little savings I had into the business. It was a risk I couldn't afford to lose at that stage," she confesses reflecting on the days of crisis. Handling the entire range of affairs, including business development, marketing, finance, production, retailing, communication or simply human resources, was all overwhelming to handle single-handedly. "If I had more funds at that stage, I would have been able to hire help and a team in all those building years," confesses Rashi talking about the first two years of business that she spent managing alone. Another big challenge Rashi faced was when she moved to Singapore with her husband in the middle of expansion and stabilizing her business.

"We had to shut down the online stores for almost a year; it was a hiccup and a scary one too. I wasn't sure if we would be able to regain our momentum." Furthermore, the responsibilities that come with married life, especially after Rashi became a mother also engaged her attention considerably.

But never once through the hurdles did it occur to the enthusiastic experimenter that she may have to give up her passion.

"You have to be persistent, keep taking small steps in the face of your challenges. Otherwise, all the effort would have been a waste," her experience speaks. Rashi was committed enough to not let the hurdles affect her, and lucky enough to have the support of friends and family.

"My husband has been my strength and support from the beginning of Heads Up For Tails. In fact, he has had faith in us ever since the first product was initiated," she relates with gratitude. What had started as a single-handed mission has become a family of fifteen members in the team and retail and online outlets, with loyal and satisfied customers across the verticals. Keeping an open ear and mind to feedback, Rashi enunciates the significance of accepting negative feedback with a positive stride.

"Oh, I am always more keen to hear the complaints than the compliments. While the latter is like a pat on the back for all the hard work, it is the former that inspires us to work on improvements. That's how we grow!" she speaks with the insight of a far-sighted entrepreneur.

Success has found its way through many doors for Rashi and her steadily growing enterprise. "One of the proudest moments for me was when we launched Heads Up For Tails in the USA this year," she states with excitement. Exemplified as a successful and ingenious entrepreneurial model, Heads Up For Tails has also been covered time and again in the leading magazines of the country.

"Earlier it was just my work and me, with the support of my family. Honestly, there had been no balance. But now that I am a mother of a two-year-old, there's much more to look out for," speaks the nurturer with the same intensity in her voice that is evident when she is talking about her enterprise. Finding the middle path between priorities of life, and working on expecting and accepting nothing less than the best in both her worlds is something Rashi has stood for in her everyday life. A true motivation for aspiring entrepreneurs, especially for women who silently nurture unfulfilled dreams, the dynamic frontrunner has showed the world how a committed and dedicated passion can bring about realization of dreams, even in the face of harshest of weathers and most unpredictable of circumstances. Standing tall with her message for all aspiring entrepreneurs to not shy away from risks but to take small yet substantial steps towards their goals, Rashi is not only making the lives of pets and their dedicated parents a better one, but also inspiring others to believe that any dream, however offbeat it may seem, has the potential of actualization.

ShubhPuja *was founded by* **Saumya Vardhan** *and aims at offering religious and astrological consultancies, helping conduct religious ceremonies and services for all occasions and needs, and providing logistical support from scratch to summary.*

The Ceremony of Success

Saumya Vardhan

The components for a prayer ceremony are beautifully laid out. The auspicious coconut on the astrologically accurate swastika and the serene, precise chanting of the vedic mantras. This ambience will remind you of a pristine temple with choicest brahmins. It is the ideal image of a desired puja proceedings. While you placidly float into this elevation, you are suddenly jolted into the reality of a poking pundit asking for more money. A ritual going clearly out of hand in terms of logistics, and what about that moment when you feel clueless in the hullabaloo around you… Sounds familiar?

This is or at least has been the dilemma of many Indians living in the country or abroad who have deep faith in religion and seek guidance on important issues and events of life through the blessings of God. Only what brushes their faces in the name of blessing is far from what they imagine. But while most people resign to this as a cultural inevitability, someone with a firm decision and a will to change perspectives took up the course of changing what religious rituals mean backstage!

Saumya Vardhan, in the first meeting, may come across as a suave management specialist who has worked and studied in

England for a better part of the last decade. She surely deserves credit for her education in business administration and finance from the Imperial College London. Additionally, accredited with Master's in Operational Research and Bachelor's in Statistics from Lady Shri Ram College also go on to speak volumes about Saumya's capability and capacity in business understanding. Experience with corporate stalwarts like KPMG and Ernst & Young are also feathers in her professional cap. Consequently, her moving back to her homeland, India and starting her own enterprise comes as no surprise. What, however, does leave them awestruck is the field of her 'business' and what drives her continual growth with every accomplished project and milestone. A proud and sensitive owner of Shubhpuja.com, Saumya has risen to achieve the position of creating a first ever online portal dedicated to organized vedic ritual services and offering science and facts based auspiciousness to people. ShubhPuja offers religious and astrological consultancies, helps to conduct religious ceremonies and services for all occasions and needs and provides logistical support from scratch to summary.

A lot of thinking and analysis has gone behind the genesis of such a unique enterprise, she explains passionately, "I only ever understood the sensitivity of the situation when a close friend's father passed away. Since all close relatives were living abroad, it became a big challenge to arrange for all rituals for the departed soul. There was no one to guide, and the family members were already in so much pain that I felt disturbed at the lack of help available."

This experience left a deep mark on Saumya's consciousness and she was drawn into creating a solution for this problem. In genuine concern for people of faith around, somewhere the idea of ShubhPuja took birth. And then there was no looking back. "I realized the irony of the situation. Here was a country that breathed the air of religious faith, and yet, no one had ever thought of making this process convenient and organized on an accessible scale!" she exclaims. Talking about the desire to do something out of the box, Saumya shares her fascination with the versatility of the country and her innate need to contribute in some way to the formation of a better society. Having assessed the need and demand of a platform that could offer quality and genuine services for Vedic rituals and guidance in matters of astrology, Saumya decided to collaborate with top Vedic educational institutes of the country to take their guidance and bring them on board with their expertise and resources. The more she researched on the issue, the deeper she realized how the faith of the ignorant masses was being exploited using the façade of unorganized services. Misinformed, pretentious and self-proclaimed preachers were minting money out of unsuspecting devotees. Soon Saumya had realized the key mantra to making this enterprise appeal to its target audience: to provide genuine and quality services, and to provide easy to access services with affordable prices. Hence, ShubhPuja emerged as a one stop solution for all religious and astrological requirements.

"We are now scientifically revolutionizing Indian traditional industry by innovating in this industry to make this easy for people to understand and follow the right scientific traditions. We are trying to make people aware of the logic and science behind these traditions that our sages have written and followed over five thousand years, instead of scaring people about their future, something most people have started doing in this industry," says Saumya shedding light on the rational element of ShubhPuja.

Going into the details of the services offered, one can be convinced of the diversity and simple consistency of ShubhPuja. "I identified the most popular types of pujas/yagnas that are conducted for everything ranging from festivals pujans to antim sanskar (last rites) pujas." Additionally, providing astrological and ritualistic solutions to specific problems of her clients became an immediate and unique edge for Saumya. On the path to revolutionize the sector of intricate services as an enterprise, ShubhPuja has now become an affordable, accessible and amicable solution available at the user's fingertip, quite literally!

But things have been more complicated than they appear for the ambitious entrepreneur.

"The risks of leaving a stable and lucrative management career to turn to something so unheard of were unimaginable for most people who I turned to for advice," she confesses candidly. "They said working with an established religious fraternity was very different from working with corporates, especially so in a country like India." But despite the strong suggestions against her idea, Saumya continued to dig deeper to make a strong case and rationalized with her family to convince them of the ingenuity and scope of the idea. Before long, she was being helped and guided by a rally of well-wishers; "They all helped to build networks and business plans, and more than anything else, they were very emotionally supportive of what I was doing," says Saumya, although she does confess to being nervous about treading unknown waters. Sharing her experiences of the initial stage, she talks about being dismissed and dwindled because of her lack of information and experience in the diocese of vedic rituals.

"I knew I had to tackle this situation head on if I wanted to survive in this race. So I enrolled myself in a course for Vedic Astrology, so that I could feel confident about what I was about to offer as a product to my clients," she declares confidently. Being able to make educated decisions about both the ritualistic as well as the logistic requirements of the products helped Saumya design packages with appropriate rates and requirements that catered to the actual needs of her current and future clients.

Along with the experience also came a new realization for ShubhPuja. That the devotees need to make educated and unbiased choices regarding their product was of key essence. To address this, Saumya brought on board some of the best educated astrologers, numerologists, and Vedic pandits. All the ceremonies and services provided are not only certified and of ensured quality, but can be explained for the rightful understanding of the clients. "I currently have a fifteen member team that comprises people educated and trained in the best institutes of the country.

"We are a strong team of pandits, astrologers, graphic designers, content writers, and business development managers. Apart from that, we have an exclusive network of highly qualified pandits/astrologers/vaastu consultants," she details with pride.

Having confidence in her enterprise comes with thorough transparency and efficiency that is taking ShubhPuja places with Saumya's endeavours. Learning and growing with every succeeding project, she accepts one of her greatest realizations, "Tying up with a top B2B client and the largest spiritual channel in the country made me understand the scale of the need and scope of ShubhPuja. Alongside also came the satisfaction that I am addressing this righteously by offering the most genuine and technology enabled solutions."

Saumya acknowledges the genesis of a revolution that will lead to completely reshaping the scenario of religious services and ceremonies in the country. "Competition lies in the small scale pandits and organizations that function locally," she analyses, "but there's no one offering such organized, accessible and genuine service, that too within the reach of a desktop, laptop or a smart phone. We definitely have an edge."

Apart from being the only organized technology based solution in the sector, ShubhPuja also claims the credit of being an exclusive one stop solution to all ritual-related needs. Additionally, with its board of experts and network of practitioners, ShubhPuja also offers credible solutions as per the needs and requirements of the client.

ShubhPuja has come a long way in its relatively short journey of about two years. In the process of building an enterprise for the service of the society, Saumya herself feels she has grown. Starting her day with prayers and gratitude for the benevolence in her life, Saumya dedicates her days to the service of strengthening the belief of other people in their faith, to support them in their times of need, both good and bad. "It's a different kind of connection we build with our clients. This perhaps has to do with the serenity and sincerity of the service that goes on in the exchange." Attributing her strength to her parents and friends who have shown undying confidence and support, Saumya reflects on her personal and professional growth as being fulfilling and inspiring. "There's a lot to be accomplished, frankly. We have only just begun taking steady steps in the journey," she proclaims, "and we are still trying to improve on our scale and accessibility."

She continues to test new waters and find out how ShubhPuja can explore and expand in new territories. "I know the television is extremely powerful and reaches every single household. That's where our real and potential consumers exist. I want to be able to use this resource to reach out to them, so they can reach out to us." Having been exposed to air time on reputed channels of the country on more than one occasion, Saumya is under no illusion about the velocity she is looking to tap. On the one hand, while she is bagging achievements one after another, the challenge of taking things forward still exists at the doorstep.

"We have been ranked number two in the top twenty-five most inspiring start-ups of the country. I have also been listed amongst the 'Top forty leading women entrepreneurs you should know about'. That sure puts ShubhPuja in the league of serious business," she calculates, still keeping check with reality. "So far I have been using my own resources and funds from my savings. But if we need to reach the scale to meet the increased demands of the product, we will need funding and promotion on a larger scale," she adds decisively. Having served and supported customers from across verticals both in India and outside, she finds relief in their vote of confidence in ShubhPuja.

"I did not have to run around to find each and every specific *puja samagri* (ingredients) and that saved me a lot of time. The package was very affordable, and the payment was extremely easy to make online. Above all, I knew the budget I had to allocate for the puja beforehand compared to traditional puja organizations. My apartment now finally feels like a home with the presence of God and positive energy in it!" expresses a very content Prashant Jha who availed the services of ShubhPuja after shifting to a new house in Gurgaon. It is testimonies like these that stand as a source of motivation for the team of ShubhPuja, which has managed to carve its niche in an otherwise stubborn and old school fraternity.

How a singular experience can be used to bring about a dynamic movement is worth learning from Saumya. Her expertise and experience, her dedication towards her service and above all, her faith in the power she endorses, has been the key to her steadily growing success. The seemingly impossible task, the seeds of which were planted two years ago, is already taking shape with strength and stability, resonating cheers and confidence of satisfaction and praises, where it spreads its wings. ShubhPuja is a vivid example of a passionate perusal of dreams and dedication to think in spaces where opportunities await to be unlocked.

Ittisa *is an only-girls digital media agency creating catchy content, exemplary designs and doing path-breaking work under founder and CEO* **Sneh Sharma**.

A Web of Women's World

Sneh Sharma

There are certain images created in the world about certain people, one's boundaries, and one's capabilities. The world, de-facto, moves along these lines of well-defined stereotypes, more often than not being caught in a comfort zone that restricts them from exploring new possibilities. One such assumption in this fast paced technology driven world is skirting around the myth that women cannot be engaged successfully in the digital space of World Wide Web marketing. While the assumption is based on the predominant male presence seen in the digital media and technology arena, the possibilities of turning the statistics around and of evolving spaces within the digital and technological dimension in favour of women are not unprecedented. One such possibility is being explored and evolved by a dynamic young leader who is running an impressive segment of the digital marketing space, defying stereotypes, statistics and suppositions alike. Sneh Sharma, currently living and working out of Bangalore is an exemplary and revolutionary entrepreneur who has redefined the digital work spectrum for women.

Sneh has been working in the space of digital media for the last seven years. Her experience has ranged from contributing to small scale start-up companies to providing backbone support for initiating what have become large enterprises. She has already established and stabilized two digital media enterprises single-handedly, all this by the young age of twenty-seven and yet, she is continuously marching towards bigger milestones of success with each step. Born and brought up in the quaint valley of Shimla in northern India, Sneh has spent a peaceful childhood in the lap of nature, the benignity and strength of which has penetrated deep into her mettle. Having absorbed all the ease of a snug life, she deliberately decided to move out of her comfort zone and moved to the dynamic city of Bangalore to pursue her MBA. Since then, determined never to slide into a state of complacence again, the technology enthusiast has been taking steady steps to explore new possibilities in different avenues.

"At the age of twenty-three, I co-founded a digital marketing firm, building it as a next generation media agency with a perfect blend of creativity, technology and analytics. However, two years into it, I was restless. I wanted to experience more and felt the urge to start over again," she exclaims with an innate burst of energy. This restlessness to make a new start, complemented by strong motivation to create a space for women in the space of digital marketing then led to the birth of Ittisa, Sneh's new and ingenious all girls' platform in the world of digital marketing. "I had read Sheryl Sandberg's sensational book *Lean In*. Not only did it inspire my entrepreneurial journey but also gave me the motivation to take a stand against the stereotype of women not being suitable for certain fields of work." Having determined her scope and shape of enterprise, the dynamic web maestro built Ittisa into what has become the only digital agency with a strong focus on design, digital and analytics along with technology.

"All our projects are creatively inspired and technically and analytically empowered," she enunciates the unique point of her web solutions. The empowerment came not only for the sake of the entrepreneurial breakthrough for Sneh; as someone who was breaking free from one shackle of convention after another, one might be tempted to believe that the initiating decisions would face challenging oppositions from the ambience. But in her case, the immediate ambience that comprised her family was anything but an opposing force. "When my mind was juggling through life-changing decisions, I was in a state of confusion and contemplation. Since I was unemployed, there was a lot of pressure. However, my family cushioned me against the stress," she candidly reveals. In the point of life when she most needed the support and acceptance of her family on the unknown path she was meaning to tread, Sneh found unconditional strength and understanding from them. It was an energy source that helped her mould the foundation of her decisions without any hesitation or opposition. Even years later into a smooth and functional regularity of her enterprise, she still returns to their love and support to find motivation in her plans of evolution, both as an enterprise as well as an individual.

Having achieved the recognition of being one of the most efficiently growing agencies in the country, Sneh and her 'super girls' make for a highly dedicated, multi-faceted and close-knit team that has evolved from a single handed lead to an eight member team with over a dozen clients in just about ten months of being operational.

However, what seems like a glorious pedestal now has been through its share of thick and thin. Being an all women agency in itself has seen its spectrum of reactions from people – both as clients and as associates. While the idea of Ittisa was initially dismissed by many as a 'far-fetched and futile idea' for being gender exclusive, the bigger challenges of business procurement and financial management were more of a concern for Sneh. "It wasn't my first time starting something from scratch; I had been exposed to the ins and outs of a business before and I was well aware of the challenges a new start-up faces, but there are unforeseen hurdles nonetheless," she admits recollecting the starting days. Finance, like in the case of most start-ups, was also a major course determining factor for Ittisa, though never a compromising one! A firm believer of turning obstructions into opportunities, Sneh has observed and moulded circumstances into her favour. To begin with, getting together an all girls' team, something that might have appeared like a challenge for many, turned out an incentive under Sneh's inspiring leadership to aspire and achieve. A traced trend of lack of trust and stability towards the young entrepreneurs proved in its own way for her to push her goals the extra mile to win the faith and confidence of her associates. "Learning to adopt, to not give in when the times are tough, is the final mantra to success in anything," she speaks with experience.

It was the initial struggle that brought the revolutionary agency to its acclamation. Within a month of their start-up, amidst building the team, strategizing and pitching to clients, Ittisa had already bagged their game-changing project with an international client from Africa. This was not only a critical achievement early in stage that helped the team evolve and expand, but also a massive wave of motivation in the face of challenges and apprehensions that the gang of girls had encountered. "Our strategy from the beginning has been not to become simply an agency for our brands, but to become their partners. We have decidedly worked as an extended arm for all our clients; we have been committed to solve real problems and help our partners grow. That's what has really worked for us," she explains with conviction. Such insight and understanding for a long term business plan comes with first-hand experience that Sneh has gained with working in different start-ups and organizations at foundation levels. Stating her predictions and decisions on the basis of her analytical capacity and experiential learnings, the passionate entrepreneur has already exhibited exemplary skills whether it is about her managerial capabilities, a bent for business understanding or technical strength that makes the backbone of her enterprise.

With a wall of support offered from friends and family, Sneh proved her worth and mettle from the initial phase itself, marking her flag with intentions of catching up in the race, and eventually leading it too.

"My parents have watched me rise and fall through the successes and failures and they have always stood by me. That's what inspires me and that's what I say to people in my team too – to stand by each other and themselves; to stick around long enough for the failures to give up before you do."

Having started the work with only two interns and a designer and the savings in her own bank account, Sneh's dynamic business skills had already rolled Ittisa into cash profit after the second month of coming into action. With immediate requirements of expansion and client acquisitions, the enterprise has evolved adequately into its current strength of ten members with profiles including marketing strategists, business developers, social media and content strategists, graphic designers and SEO analysts. Having crossed the milestone of one crore rupees within seven months of operation, this assumed underdog has acquired and retained over twenty clients in its current portfolio, all of whom are impressed with the exclusive dedication of Ittisa in its attention to design, analytics and technology, all at once in the digital space.

Talk about what she plans next and the futuristic strategist has all her ideas aligned into place, "The digital space is continually evolving, carrying with it immense potential for growth, and that growth is happening with a strong mix of creativity with technology and analytics. CMOs are not only going digital but also becoming more technical." Tapping into the market opportunity, Sneh is set on expansions in the three hot dimensions of marketing – digital, mobile and wearable. With a keen sense of the trends and evolution in her field, the avid learner sticks true to her desire of constantly improving and progressing both as a high rising enterprise as well as a person who is passionate about her growth. "I see this as a true reflection of all my aspiration," she reveals, "I constantly look out for windows of opportunities, of corrections and improvements – that's my ultimate drive and motivation." Sharing the same spirit even in her personal life, the woman who wheels the organization maintains the equilibrium that takes to strengthen her personal life. At home, she is also a dedicated contributor in her family affairs. In her companionship with her friend and husband Bhupendra, Sneh finds true care, critique and complacence all at the same time. As two individuals who complement each other, both Sneh and Bhupendra run their own enterprises and are seen to stand strong for each other whether at home or in the work space. Sharing responsibilities, doing chores together, taking decisions together or simply connecting about issues of work is a mutual act of affection and understanding between the duo. "In my personal life, just as in my profession, I am blessed to be in a state of perfect abundance of success, people and happiness," she exhilarates with a humble hint of pride. At this point in life Sneh is looking ahead at a road that heads only uphill. There's no place in the world she'd rather be.

What had once started amidst the clouds of intriguing uncertainties and trepidations has now become a destination that most seek and follow without any doubts. In an arena where an all-women's organization was a distant imagination with little ground to hold, today Ittisa stands as a statement of its own identity, redefining work suitability, capability and adaptability of a woman. In the digital world, Sneh has bootstrapped an inimitability which was once a taboo but now holds as strength, supporting Ittisa to stand out from the crowd. Churning, what was an intimidating weakness, into a dedicated and motivated strength with her multi-dimensional and talented team of women, she has paved the way for many aspiring women and men to overcome their apprehensions and break stereotypes.

If you wish to make a mark for yourself in the digital world, visit www.ittisa.com.

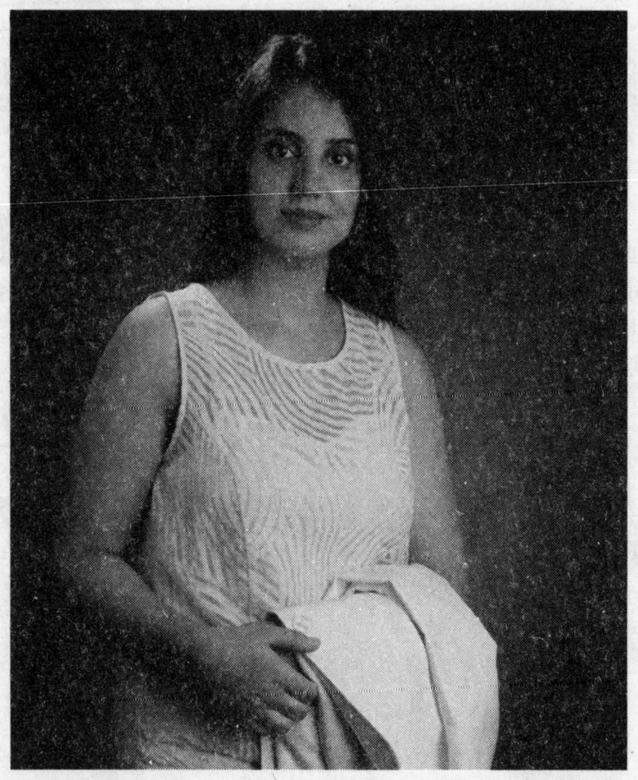

Dr Surbhi Mahajan *was inspired to found* **Dermatocare** *to offer skin care solutions that are accessible and affordable, and provide free consultation sitting at home.*

Beauty beyond Skin

Surbhi Mahajan

Every morning, she wakes up early and begins her day with some brisk walking, peaceful meditation and chanting, and a hurried dedication to the chores of a typical family household. Towards the end of the day, she is found spending quality time with her four-year-old son and chatting with her husband. What may seem like an average day in every Indian woman's life is actually filled with power-packed activities between the morning chores and evening family chitter-chatter. For Surbhi, life breathes with a conscious, philanthropic and ambitious air.

An inquisitive scholar and researcher, a dermatology consultant by profession and an entrepreneur by passion, Surbhi Mahajan holds an MBBS degree and is a university topper. More than merely acquiring and delivering educational learning, she has redefined medical consultation and brought down skin care solution in a responsible and reachable system to its seeker. Having worked as a dermatologist in the early stages of her career path, Surbhi has been exposed to the various facets of skin care and has been deeply aware of the discrepancies – systemic or unintentional.

"I was regularly bombarded with categorical questions about the best skin care products, best treatment methods, homemade remedies for skin types, etc." she explains in reminiscence of the early days. Finding genuine and specific solutions to diverse skin care problems was the only agenda in her head for months at a stretch.

"Medical schools don't teach you the answers to such real-life questions that arise in people's minds. That is why I felt this urgent need to dive deep into research and experimentation to figure out the answers myself," she adds. Being up to date with information available online and through experts and research papers from across the world, Surbhi was more and more convinced with the fact that the skin care industry was being driven by false claims. "Making you look five years younger with a simple cream instantly has more to do with expert make-up and onscreen editing than the miracles of medicine. And once I had figured this out, I knew I had to find an authentic and unbiased solution for skin problems," she expresses.

What began with a quest for right answers regarding rising skin care dissatisfaction and sheer philanthropic motivation, purposefully turned into an organized blog for skin care advice with democratic access to readers. Information ranging from basic skin type information to more intricate details of both homemade and medical remedies were available free of cost for all of Surbhi's readers. Needless to say, the response was unprecedented! Viewers flocked to the blog with queries, concerns and eventually, feedback. Rightly so, because this was the first time free consultation on skin care solutions was being offered online, open to anyone's access, and that too, free of cost. What Surbhi had to ensure and observe continually was that the information being sought and offered was relevant, accurate and feasible for the users. "One thing I have learnt and emphasized over the years is that each person has very unique skin requirements and situations that need to be handled with personal attention and understanding. Mass solution cannot be appropriated to address this individual issue," she rationalizes. Letting her research speak for this concept, Surbhi went to the length of designing and generating questionnaires to understand each skin type to be able to effectively provide solutions to her readers. Before long, the occasional blogging had taken over as an unconventional online portal with professional medical aid, with its genesis in 2012 as Dermatocare.com. Offering online consultation, Q&As, and access to genuine, authentic product information, all this free of cost, speaks volumes of the dedication behind creating such a platform.

In an attempt to break the commercial run through of cosmetic giants, Dermatocare has been dedicating personal attention to each and every seeker, follower or eventual seeker with only the most relevant and plausible answers to the skin care solutions they seek. Surbhi ensures that every question, before being answered, or product, before being endorsed, is matched best with the situation of the client. "There is the basic, advanced and expert form of recommendation we make to our clients on the basis of their problem, availability of time, the money they can invest, and importantly, their willingness to take dermatological consultation with intent," she explains categorically. Having studied the user pattern for many years now, Surbhi is confident in explaining the driving phenomenon that governs the model of Dermatocare.

"Many patients don't step into a dermatologist's clinic, but might try remedies at home or salons. Dermatocare strives to guide them, with researched and easy to follow tips and natural skin care solutions."

With this insight, the step by step process of Dermatocare attempts to build faith in its customers by understanding their needs, offering them solutions that are accessible and affordable, and providing free consultation sitting at home. Once this relationship has been built, consumers are encouraged to try credible and relevant products and meet consultants in clinics for advance treatments or further care.

"Most brands of beauty and skin care are offering glamourous and short-term solutions to the more deeply embedded problems of dermatological issues. We are striving to break that pattern so people can find realistic and authentic alternatives. In the process, we try our best to promote solutions that are safe and healthy, both for themselves and for the environment," Surbhi discusses with complete faith in this slow but steady process.

So how does this philanthropic platform really operate, one may wonder. Beginning with an extremely well-researched questionnaire, the customers are given accurate information regarding their skin, its advantages, issues and risks. On the basis of this analysis, free online consultation is provided related to the best care practices, useful products, 'dos and don'ts' for different skin types, etc. Only once these services have been availed does the business generation plan comes in with paid consultation for detailed and advanced solutions, with expert dermatologists on-board Dermatocare.

Over the past years of its development, Dermatocare has formed a strong consumer ship and faith amidst its clients and a sincere and dedicated team of dermatologists from across the country on its panel for consultation. But things haven't been as easy as the click and scroll virtual clinic that Dermatocare offers its users on the web. "Things were extremely challenging and unpredictable in the beginning. To leave the course of a stable consultation job and start something online was not an easy initiative," Surbhi confesses. From paranoia over web services to opposition of offering free consultancy as professional suicide, she witnessed it all. On days of good research and positive feedback, she'd find inspiration to cross over the challenging ones that were filled with doubt and reflections on whether she was headed in the right direction or not. "I was a dermatologist before we started out with this venture. Now I am an entrepreneur, a leader, a blogger and it has indeed been an enriching journey," says Surbhi. From mastering communication techniques on the World Wide Web to understanding business and team management, Dermatocare also sheds light on the story of how it has helped her grow as a human being. Her encounter with her inner, truer self, her brush with the door of spirituality and her ultimate surrender to faith are some of the priceless achievements that Surbhi counts as her takeaways from her journey this far. "I had a three-year-old son, and my husband had just moved to Jakarta. I was in the process of building up Dermatocare in a strange country all by myself. I was facing the most humbling test of my strength at this stage," she recalls with shimmering eyes. Being introduced to the *Bhagwad Gita* through a friend's recommendation came as a blessing for Surbhi. This not only brought her closer to her faith but also helped her find connection to her spiritual self. "I have been very blessed in my life. To have a husband who is so supportive, to be surrounded by well-wishers as friends and family who stand by me, and most importantly, to be spiritually aware and connected to the almighty is what has been the mantra to my happiness and strength all these years," she adds serenely.

Also attributing to this steady success is a cooperative and understanding team of members that Surbhi fondly talks about. "There are four crucial members that help me as a team, and they are the pillars of support. While I handle the concept and content that goes into building Dermatocare, my staff takes care of marketing, web designing, developing and SEO," she shares proudly. Although confessing that it becomes challenging to see that all targets are delivered on time, and to coordinate across panels transcending geographies, the founder of Dertmatocare does believe in constantly aiming for improvement and pushing boundaries to compete with her own benchmarks of success.

"It's important that I set examples with my own actions," she adds, "only then can I expect others to follow and feel the need to do better."

With such appreciable growth in the last three years, Dermatocare has managed to feature some of the best skin specialists in the country and to be endorsed by some of the most prominent names in the industry. But for Surbhi, there's no pausing on this long walk ahead. "Frankly speaking, I still think we're way behind our goals. Currently we are working on improving user experience on the website because that is our direct point of contact with our customers and we need to ensure it's designed in the most user-friendly and efficient manner to help them." Her meaningful eyes reflect someone who is intent on achieving nothing short of perfection. Talking about the competition in the market, Surbhi bullets out the risks and opportunities she has listed out in her marketing strategies. "Beauty bloggers, natural skin care channels and skin care information websites are our direct competitors in the web-space. But they either don't offer details of products, ingredients and skin information that we do, instead they offer mass advice for all problems. We take pride in detailed, personalized solutions that cater to individual issues," she talks about the edge she believes Dermatocare has over her competitors. Having planned her objective targets over the next years, Surbhi delves deep into her research on her fast-increasing knowledge of web-based communication. Though it may not be an area of expertise for her, the fact does not deter Surbhi from expanding her knowledge and experience in all parallel fields that may help her make Dermatocare more efficient and successful in its services.

With one short pause into the conversation, and a quick phone call, she is back diving into web pages, studying the latest report of research on aloe vera, with half a smile over something her son had told her over the phone. Juggling between a delicate domestic life and a demanding enterprise, Surbhi is truly an example of a powerful woman who is creating a beautiful balance in all spheres of her life. She admits that being a working woman in Jakarta is safer and more empowered than it was back at home, but she does believe that one's conviction and passion can inspire all the strength one needs. "I always see women around me being apprehensive of taking up their own work because they don't want to compromise with the family. I always tell them that on the contrary, it helps to bring independence and understanding that'll make you feel stronger and more motivated to balance all shades of your life."

Wrapping up her day in the office, Surbhi lets in on the secret to her success. "It doesn't lie in the numbers of hits my site gets or list of clients that add to our list. It is in the joy of watching people finding the confidence about themselves and in going to bed every night knowing that the smiles we have brought on people's faces are not false promises, but true experiences they can relish." As she steps out to meet her husband to take a walk to the garden, an air of satisfaction lingers behind in the room. It is a feeling that inspires one to not only build a dream, but to know that the strength to follow the dream also lies within. Surbhi's skin care solutions may be lightening up the outer beauty of many people in the world, but they truly reveal the inner beauty she radiates in the cause she has taken up, in both her career and philosophy of her life.

Tina Garg *is the founder of* **Pink Lemonade**, *a creative agency specializing in communication, content, and design.*

A Refreshing Taste of Creation!

Tina Garg

You never know where life leads you to. You might have planned something, but end up in an entirely different scenario. Sometimes, when you haven't penned things down in ink, and let your life find its own natural course, you chance upon the most beautiful and meaningful journey that you were destined to make. For those who ignore this natural phenomenon, life is a disappointing mystery full of hurdles, negativity, and unexplained changes. On the other hand, if someone listens to their calling, explores paths without fearing the consequences and their inner voice, he or she discovers great heights of exploration, evolution and accomplishment. Such lives – creative, expressive and inspirational in their nature – often make great stories for people to share and learn from.

One such simple yet significant story echoes from the life and light of a woman dynamic in her voracity, passionate in her creativity, and daring in her fecundity. Tina Garg, with her free and dedicated spirit surpassed all predictions of convention to give shape to her dreams and put together a workforce that not only stands strong for its exemplary quality of output, but also makes it worth a look for its redefined attitude towards creativity and communication. From deciding her own career graph in the field of creative expression to creating an entire organization that leads with creative definition, Tina has come a long way with her aspirations. On this path, she stands today with an innovative, attractive and effective agency known as Pink Lemonade. Operational for five years now, the creative hub operates out of the vibrant city of Bangalore. Dedicated to all disciplines of creative advertising and marketing, Tina's enterprise has evolved efficiently in all fields. Within a short period of time, the venture has already acquired a clientele of about 250 brands, many of which include the top names of the country.

What seems to be a stable, strengthened organization today has its roots in several turns of fate and hard work. The young Tina of a few years ago may have seemed like any other engineer in the field of computer science.

"Even while I was in the tech field, I knew my interest lingered in writing and communication. One way or another, I was always connected with various forms of expression," she explains. From writing in publications for college to actively making an academic choice and taking up diploma courses in creative writing in London, to having defined her concrete decision to continue in the field with Master's in Marketing and Communications, the young scholar remained conscious of her calling and chose her course of action accordingly. Even during her years as an employee with various organizations, Tina's experience strengthened in content and tech-marketing, social sector communication, and design and content for creative agencies. The avid writer utilised her flair for professional writing as a freelancer even after becoming a mother and went on to publish about three hundred by-lines in mainstream publications within a period of two years. Not only was her efficient talent in communication evident, but her dedication and commitment as a writer has been worthy of acknowledgement.

Speaking of the advent of the '.com' culture in India, Tina explains having tapped the industry at the opportune moment.

"E-commerce was just about beginning to spread its wings in the country back then and I got a chance to work with the best brand in Bangalore, heading a team of 350 writers across the country and curating content for the web portal."

This was an experience of both inspiration and insight for the ground-breaking thinker and eventually led to a gradual realization that helped formulate her brainchild – Pink Lemonade. Working for several companies as a consultant gradually butterflied into her thinking of her own enterprise, one that amalgamated both her passion for business as well as communication.

"They say do what you love and you will never work for a day! I think the saying fits me perfectly. The joy of ideating, creating and defining new communication expressions every single day is both effortless and refreshing. That's how I know I am doing the right thing," she reveals candidly.

Speaking fondly of her enterprise, Tina explains the concept of Pink Lemonade as an agency specializing in content, communication and design; one that offers end-to-end solutions such as corporate identity creation, marketing collateral, internal communication, environment space branding, web design services, video scripting, editing and production. However, in the advertising and marketing industry, these services are more or less offered by a plethora of agencies. Then what makes Pink Lemonade so different, one might wonder.

"The ethos in the organization is its most special quality. We're not here for a mere commercial transaction. We're an agency with a heart. I firmly believe that if one's motivation and inspiration is satiated, then quality, performance and delivery will all excel automatically."

The same freshness of mood, creativity of thoughts and attitude for work resonates clearly in the name of her enterprise that believes in shedding conventional ideas and methodologies and working on their own style of communication, like the lemonade with a pink twist – exciting and effective all at once!

The lively, chirpy woman expresses her appreciation for the people around her – friends and family, who have inspired her to learn and grow through the journey of being an entrepreneur. An admirer of the women who have taken the plunge and made examples of themselves, Tina herself believes in grabbing every opportunity and giving it her own creative, effective blend.

"Every day in the creative field is like delivering a baby – when something that you have worked for hours to create finally gets done, it's a great joy!" she speaks fondly about Pink Lemonade. However, the realist does not shy away from speaking of the problems that came with the dream. As a woman entrepreneur in a predominantly male space, Tina encountered her own set of challenges. "I knew the climb would be steeper because I am a woman. There were times when I had to struggle hard to be taken seriously, to establish my own space in the industry." The genesis was a crucial phase that Tina attended to with utmost sincerity and consideration. From the time the switch came from working for herself to business through an entire organization, she devoted time picking and designing the best team, the best processes and the best policies that would go on to define the future of the enterprise. All this needed a strong team and funds, both of which were not easy to find and filter. But the optimist always took on challenges as opportunities of evolution and built herself an enterprise that prides itself today in its people and work philosophy. Ask the self-made leader what her key to success is, and she humbly accredits her family, team, and husband for the crucial roles they have played in this endeavour. "My husband, Tapan, runs his own business and his mentorship has been one of the key strengths for Pink Lemonade. From initiation to stabilization and expansion, he has been extremely supportive throughout our journey."

After the initial lessons and experiences, Pink Lemonade has established itself as a stable presence, with progress coming easily and effectively. "Within the last two years, we have seen such a sharp rise in the business that it amazes me. Consequently, we have expanded in strength, both in quality and quantity," she speaks with pride. This sense of achievement has also come with a lot of insightful perseverance. Tina's attention has been focused as much on the input that the organization gets as the output it produces. Her innovation and sensitivity have had a strong hand in the formation of a productive culture at the workplace. Through initiatives that are smart and effective, Pink Lemonade has become a place where people like to come and contribute every day. By creating an environment that encourages ingenuity and ownership, she has helped nurture individuals and transform them into leaders who are responsible, creative, and passionate in their attitude towards their goals. The team has grown in capacity and numbers and has diversified into expertise of the web, copy, design and client servicing – four areas of advertising that Pink Lemonade claims it specializes in.

However, the efficiency that Pink Lemonade swears by is not merely limited to its workplace. Elements of personal aspirations are addressed and nurtured here in this hub of creativity.

"Pink Lemonade strongly encourages people to have a good life outside the work space." While work efficiency is expected to be optimum in most organizations, this is a unique workforce that actually does something to encourage productivity and well-being of its employees. Innovative concepts such as 'Pink Holiday' – a sponsored day off for an employee through monthly draws, fun Fridays and awards for performance, and in addition, celebration of birthdays add a personal touch to the professional environment. "We believe in providing equal opportunity and encouragement to all our employees. This specially reaches out to women who have a tough time balancing their family and office needs," Tina adds with sensitivity. With their 'never say no' attitude, the employees of Pink Lemonade have formed impression in the industry for their will and commitment to the best. Many clients have been known to speak in praise of the agency not only in words but also in loyalty.

"I have already put Pink Lemonade under my list of 'go to' people for any design work that I would need," says a very happy client from a software company. While maintaining their own creative spirit and uniqueness, Pink Lemonade is known for its 'go-getter' attitude that enables them to push the envelope and go that extra mile in their performance. The head of a top multinational brand does not hesitate from evaluating the agency's excellence in fond words. "As a client, when judging any ad agency, I always look at parameters such as their ability to understand our requirement, understand the big picture, be flexible, turnaround things fast, and have a good design sense and well-crafted content that is relevant to the TA. Of course, all this at a cost that fits our budget! Pink Lemonade team and their 'can-do' attitude is something that I love!"

Ask the calm-headed founder about her own attitude to work and she gives you a gentle yet generous smile. "I believe in simple and effective things in life. As long as your approach is sincere and well meant, everything turns out perfectly well, whether it's work or personal life," she explains her philosophy. A huge fan of cooking exotic recipes, Tina loves making chocolate at home for her family. The one that has determined and designed the present of such an incredible organization is also an enthusiastic tarot card reader in her free time. As someone who has scheduled minutes on her calender, Tina is extraordinarily well balanced when it comes to her family. "While work is important, I make it a point to be there for my family and not miss out on my kids' growing up years. I believe that I have a huge spiritual presence in my life which keeps me grounded and holds me together in the trying times," she adds with serenity.

Being content and yet constantly evolving is the mantra that keeps the voracious creator going. Irrespective of the challenges and competition, Tina believes in striving for excellence of the self, instead of getting stuck in the limitations of comparatives. "That would be an easy thing to do," she explains, "but when I am on my own journey, to find my own excellence, I think success and prosperity will follow as companions, not as a greed I have to hungrily pursue." As someone who has set an example for many in the rat race of advertising, Tina is a symbol of holistic creativity – someone who is not driven by mere ambition of material achievements, but creative and spiritual well-being. She encourages all aspiring entrepreneurs to embrace challenges and overcome limitations with an open perspective towards learning. With these lessons in mind, she says, anyone can reach the pinnacle of personal and professional achievement in their lives.

Vidula Kantikar Kothare *is the co-founder of* **Think Creative AdSolutions Pvt Ltd**, *which provides end to end solutions for marketing, advertising, branding, event management, among others.*

Advertising a Balanced Life!

Vidula Kanitkar Kothare

More than two decades ago, an art teacher in Mumbai was advising a set of parents to let their daughter pursue a career in art, a thought very far-fetched and seemingly impractical at that time for the humble Brahmin couple. Nobody in the family had taken up the field of art as a serious career choice. There were apprehensions through the years, but the teacher's recommendation resonated through the little girl's mind all along. Many years later, a young and dynamic woman walked into the world of creativity with an aspiration to mark her own niche. Vidula Kanitkar Kothare was no commoner to follow trends, nor has she stopped taking risks and doing what feels right in her heart. It is this attribute that has led her to become one of the youngest woman entrepreneurs to find recognition in the field of creative advertising.

Starting with endeavours dating back to the year 2002, Vidula first made up her mind and will to set up an independent enterprise to unleash her creative mettle into the promising realm of communications in marketing and advertising. Strengthening her interest with educational expertise, she studied Applied Art and a dedicated specialization in Digital Media from reputed institutes in Mumbai. Further gaining experience with some advertising agencies helped her form the base of what later became a well-rooted career.

"I always knew I would be doing something independent eventually. While working in other organizations, I had noted my strength in selling my creative ideas to people, and in coming up with out of the box ideas, some of which I used in small scale freelance work that I engaged in alongside," explains a retrospective Vidula, "and soon I realized it would be more productive and lucrative to start something of my own."

This realization, along with the destined company of her then closest friends led to forming a group, freelancing together in Mumbai in the then small industry of ad solutions. Recollecting the early days of her struggle, she talks about working out of home and sharing sleepless nights trying to prepare pitches for hard to get clients. "There was this particular assignment we were working on for a potentially big client when the only computer system we had crashed!" she explains candidly. "With few choices, we sought help which came in the form of a blessing through Mr. Tushar Dhote, a leading printer in Mumbai who offered us his machine and office space to get the work done. We finished that assignment in less than twenty-four hours and impressed our clients enough that they came back for more! That was when we knew for sure we were headed to form a company of our own, set it up formally and kick start work in full form." This, in principle, was the genesis of Think Creative AdSolutions Private Limited.

A creative agency that stands for more than just out of the box thinking, Think Creative is known amidst its existing and loyal clients for the dedicated and sincere solutions it offers. "We believe in simple but effective solutions. Whatever creatives we come up with has to do justice to the brand in terms of its visibility and sales in the market, not merely in completing the task. We always keep our strengths and capabilities clear to our clients," Vidula explains with sincerity, the unique attraction of her agency in being genuine and honest – to themselves and to their clients. With a valley of experience to their credit, Think Creative has evolved with dedicated relations with each of its clients. This rare phenomenon helps them stand out amidst the rapid race between mushroomed agencies.

Acclaimed clients have expressed their first encounter with the agency as being heart-warming, cooperative and extremely meticulous. "I spent some days in the office of Think Creative and observed that every single client received personal attention and support." Through the years of establishing themselves as a dedicated organization, the founders of Think Creative – Nikhil, Hitesh and Vidula – have learnt with humility and established their credibility with sustained clients and consistent growth on the basis of a foundation built with experience.

It would be a mistake to assume that all this happened like a dream coming true without road blocks or reality checks.

"It was difficult to be taken seriously by people (back then when we just started) around me, even family members, let alone clients," confesses Vidula. Even experiences in the ad world were not so smooth in the beginning for the three novices, she recalls.

"The brands judged our potential on the basis of our under-aged appearances. It took a lot of convincing to make them understand our potential. This made us work twice as hard." The challenges varied from trying to put together a team as work increased, to stumbling into the nuances of the skills of a business. "I have a creative inclination, but as a woman in business, it is critical to understand the finance and marketing sides of a creative agency," she continues. The young founder goes on to explain how the initial years were accompanied by offers from bigger organizations to buy them, and recalls particularly her brush with the aggressive tactics of the industry. "In our initial years, there was an upcoming marketing company that outsourced their creative requirements to us. One of the guys associated with that company was a leading creative director from the advertising industry. After almost a year of using our services, one fine day he just started rejecting all our work, declaring our incapability and questioning the credibility of our staff," Vidula talks about the attempts at sabotaging her spirit and confidence. "That was the tipping point for me. That incident really hit me hard as a challenge to prove my worth." Proving her point with effective solutions, the passionate artist revels in simplicity and relevance which, to her mind, can take communication a long way ahead. "Our guiding mantra just goes on to speak for itself because we have managed to survive and expand. That marketing agency however, shut down years ago," she absorbs the learning that has stuck with her over the years, feeling grateful for the eye-opening lesson.

Learning from such challenges, Think Creative has endeavoured to step up to make themselves approachable and trustworthy – qualities known to transcend limitations of age or apprehensions. Analyzing how to evaluate creativity and apply adequate resources for each project are some of the lessons learnt in the process. Taking calculated risks in business is what she strongly believes in. Identifying a relationship with the client as the key to succeeding in any enterprise, she recalls starting out with some clients with disagreements and arguments. But keeping her ears and mind open to feedback and patiently investing in building a relation with them has helped her come a long way,

"The same set of people are now my most consistent and satisfied clients because I learnt to listen to their perspectives, and understand their needs to help build my solutions for them."

As a leader for her team of fifteen young and dynamic minds, Vidula talks about the importance of keeping a few steps ahead. Along with diversifying into various sectors for their portfolio, she also encourages her team to read up and understand about all verticals that include the network of existing or potential clients. "Every opportunity to know and learn should be grabbed. Which is why every time we come across a good campaign or idea, we sit and discuss it as a team and let it inspire us," she explains dismissing the idea of competition in the sector. "You will have competitors in every industry. The key is to learn from the environment and compete with excellence in you." Living every word her organization stands for, she encourages her team to connect all thought processes and pour them into their creative mettle.

"Hence the name Think Creative fits our motto perfectly," she adds excitedly.

Emphasizing on the work culture that promotes productivity and creativity, Vidula expresses her belief in the economic and justified use of time. "I strongly believe that most of our work that needs to be done can be completed within office hours." With a strict weekend off policy, Think Creative has grown in providing services that not only exceed expectations for the clients but also bring great gratification for the team involved in delivering it. Enunciating the necessity to keep balance between life in and outside work, Vidula encourages and practices the same even in her own life.

Married to her work pillar, quite literally, Vidula talks about her partner and husband Nikhil who is not only a symbol of support for her in keeping the enterprise stand tall, but also an encouraging and compassionate life partner. She explains his crucial role in having identified and accepted her strengths and weaknesses as a business partner and working around it for the best. Juggling her personal and professional conundrums, Vidula strives to perfection in her life at home just as it is at work. "There's a lot expected of a woman who steps into enterprising dimensions. I am aware of that. But with the right attitude and determination, it's possible to celebrate and excel all the aspects of being a woman. Each and every role that a woman plays in her life has to be given full justice. Be it as a wife, a daughter, a boss in office or a mother at home – she has got to be perfect at each of these. But the most important role for me is being a mother. Motherhood has taught me a lot and gives me immense strength to get through every single day. I strive to be a true inspiration for my child."

Identifying women as multi-tasking geniuses, she revels in the true strength of being a woman who, as an individual is capable of independence, strength, responsibility and leadership. In doing so, however, Vidula does acknowledge the unconditional support and understanding she has received from her family, specially her mother Bhavana Kanitkar and father Bhalchandra Kanitkar, who inspire her to be a dedicated and loving mother in turn to her child Vihaan. Equally supporting have been her in-laws, she declares, in helping her find a symphonic ease in becoming the successful woman she is today.

With humility as a guiding virtue, Vidula appreciates and acknowledges all the support she has received from her family and colleagues in the dream she had built as a rising entrepreneur. More importantly, absorbing life and its experiences as valued teachers, she keeps an open mind for all mistakes and lessons that help her grow both personally and professionally. Keeping all the feathers in her cap close for inspiration, she remembers even the little milestones she has crossed in this journey. "Everything holds significance. Whether it was our registration as a private limited company, our first retainer client or our first international client, they all have been opportunities to be proud of and to learn from," she smiles with happiness reflecting in her eyes. The dynamic artist has featured on forums like ETV Marathi as the young achiever, and on the internet as 'successful women entrepreneur of the month' on a popular website on women entrepreneurs. She firmly believes that while these have been moments to relish, her real goal is in bringing Think Creative to its full potential, expanding across cities and countries.

An overwhelmingly occupied Vidula starts her day at her work desk with what she calls the 'challenges of the day' with a determination to convert them into solutions before the end of the office hours. She remains positive and strongly believes whatever happens, happens for the best.What started in a borrowed space with an array of creative ideas, three determined young friends, an operating system and zero budget has today actualized into a destination that many brands return to for their advertising and marketing solutions. Defying conventions, both on personal and professional fronts, Vidula is an example for many young aspirants who find themselves intimidated and confused in the sea of a giant industry. With perseverance, honesty and sincerity as her key weapons, the gifted creative head of Think Creative has won the hearts of not only her clients but also contemporaries who have witnessed her strength and passion through this journey. Walking to and from her desk in an engaged conversation with one of her clients, Vidula exonerates herself from any other distraction that may hinder her thoughts in the particular moment. Relaying assignments between tasks and teams, she moves closer to her solutions, thinking meticulously about her challenges and putting her art to work for the rest of the world to see.

Upcoming title by the same author

The Better-Halves of Start-Ups

In an era booming with the 'Start-Up' trend and loving this new attitude of breaking boundaries and conventions of a career, one also meets the challenge of being able to partner up with the right people. In lieu of reliable and trustworthy partners, real life couples in relationships have started exploring the idea of partnering up in business too!

Many start-ups today have been ideated and built by couples, who either studied together, have been married or have dwelled in the same environment. Having known each other for a considerably long time and watched each other through different circumstances, gives a certain advantage of understanding and acceptance. As a result, such partnerships compile with a greater degree of acceptability and support.

Aparna and Vinay, co-founders of GreenNGood, have been married for several years now and have been successfully leading their brand.

Vishal, co-founder of ArtZolo, recalls his initial stages of entrepreneurial hiccups and how his wife and co-founder Preeti helped him get out of it.

Akriti and Anshul, co-founders of Boring Brands have worked with each other through a plethora of projects.

Speaking to various couples in the country who have come together as business partners, one realizes that the myth about mixing work and home is just as misty as the one about needing a stable and conventional job for an ambitious career. When great minds come together to produce something built on conjoined dreams, the result is eminently successful, lucrative and deeply satisfying.

The Better-Halves of Start-Ups brings out such lovely stories of enterprising couples. #Readon.